Science of Magic Book 1

By

Meredith Spies

Additional Credits:

DEVELOPMENTAL EDITS: Charlie Knight (CKnight Writes)

Editing by M.A. Hinkle (LesCourt Author Services)

Beta Reading by Kirk Waite (LesCourt Author Services)

Proof Reading by Lori Parks (LesCourt Author Services)

Cover Art and Promotional Art by Samantha Santana (Amai Designs)

Prologue

ORRIN

Twenty Years Ago

He looks wrong.

I rose up onto my toes and peered down at Dad. His color was odd, and the way his mouth was shaped created a smile unlike his own. Dad's smile made his eyes crinkle up and his nose do this squishy thing, dimpling his cheeks like mine. This version was flat and looked weird. Like he was trying to squeeze his lips together too hard. Slowly,I reached out brushed a finger across the too-smooth cheek. No one stopped me, so I rubbed his skin, trying to feel the bristles that never seemed to go away even after he put foam all over his face.

"He's cold."

In the murmur and rustle of the strange party, my voice was lost. Dad said my voice was tiny sometimes, and I guess that was why no one heard me. Thick carpet muffled everyone's steps, and the benches and chairs were padded with a weird, squeaky plastic, meant to look like leather. It made too much noise, this room, and it made it hard to hear anything other than the carpet-chair-clothes sounds, like bird feathers brushing together.

Mom wasn't where I'd left her, sitting on one of the squeaky bench things. I saw a bunch of strangers, though, and some people who worked with Dad. Most of the strangers were reporters. When we went on Fun Days to the park or museum without Mom, I could remember Dad smiling for some reporters. They always had weird recorders like some of the strangers here did.

I looked back at Dad, lying in the dull gray box. Mom brought me with her to pick it out, and the man had called it the Eternal Rest model.

I tried to feel the mattress inside, but Mom had yelled, and I'd cried, and we'd left.

Dad didn't look comfortable, not if his smile was wrong.

His smile was wrong, and he felt wrong, and he even smelled wrong. It wasn't my dad in the Eternal Rest bed. Dad wouldn't stay in a stupid box and act wrong. The weird place was a bad place, and I wanted to leave *right away please,* but no one would listen to me.

"It's not him. He looks wrong. This isn't him."

Someone shushed me. "Where's Eloise?" they asked no one in particular. "What's he doing here by himself?"

I touched Dad's face again, pressing gently against his cheek. "It's not him. He feels like a candle or something."

Hands I didn't know scooped me up and carried me quickly away. "Let's go see if they have any cookies in the other room, huh? Doesn't that sound good?"

"Not really. Where's my dad?" I twisted and turned, trying to see who was carrying me. I wasn't supposed to go with strangers anywhere, and Dad would be so upset if I did. After the time the weird guy tried asking me questions at Astroworld, he made me promise. "That's not him. This isn't funny!"

I tried to kick my legs, but the man holding me squeezed, keeping them still. Something in my chest and tummy rattled around, banging on my ribs and making it hard to breathe. Dad was in the Eternal Rest bed, and I couldn't find Mom, and people were giving me sad face looks, and I wanted my Dad to stop messing around *now*.

The man holding me pushed open some doors, and that thing in my chest hit *hard*. If we went through the doors, I'd be far from my dad, and I needed to keep an eye on him, to see when he'd stop playing this trick. "Let me go!"

"It's..." The man didn't finish the sentence, and I knew why. He was going to tell me it's okay or something. He was going to lie to me, and I hated him. Twisting again, I got a leg loose, kicking him in the stomach until he finally set me down. "Let's get you some water."

"No!"

"Where the hell is Eloise?" he muttered, reaching past me to close the office door. The room smelled bad, like that air freshener Grandma used in the bathroom mixed with wet dog. There was a big couch on one side of the room and a desk on the other. A whole bunch of boxes of tissues stood against the wall, as if someone wanted to make a fort. "Here, let's have a seat, okay?" The man smiled at me, but it was fake. Not the same way Dad's was, but like he was trying to be happy but wasn't.

"I want to go check on Dad," I said, even though that thing in my chest wanted to choke me. "He's wrong."

The man rubbed his eyes the way I did when I wanted to cry. "Your dad was...he's my friend." He squatted down in front of me so we were almost the same height. "We've worked together a long time, since high school!"

"High school is for big kids. I'm not a big kid yet."

He laughed, and it was watery, like he was gurgling on it. "No, not yet. Your dad and I met when we were big kids, though. Here." He pulled out a tiny ball from his coat pocket, like the kind from gumball machines Mom wouldn't let me get because she was afraid I'd try to eat them. "Your dad used to do a magic trick with one of these. Did he ever show you?"

Nodding, I grinned, showing him my teeth because Dad said that was my best smile, the happiest one. "He could move it without his hands!"

The man nodded too. "Can you do that, too?"

I grinned again. "Yep. Put it down and I can show you."

The man set the ball on the floor and duck-walked back a few feet, almost to the tissue-box wall. He made a little wave with his hand, like "go on." The same way Mom sometimes did when I was walking too slow.

My Spider-Man light up shoes didn't want to come off until I kicked at them really hard. "Don't let me lose those. Mom will be so mad. They're my special shoes 'cause they light up." I went to stand in front of the ball. "Look!" I stretched out a leg and curled my toes around it, scooting it back toward me. "Taa-daa!"

He stared at me for a long time. Then that smile was back, but real this time. He giggled, sounding funny like it got stuck in his throat. He fell on his butt and pressed his hands over his face.

I didn't like hide and seek much, but sometimes you needed to hide, I guess.

I sat on the floor with the ball, rolling it back and forth between my feet. "You okay? I want to go back to Dad now." That thing in my chest rolled around again. "I think maybe I can help him. He looks wrong. Maybe he just needs to know I'm there and it's not funny."

He stopped hiding his face. "Your dad." He nodded at the ball between my feet. "He used to do that same joke at work, when people asked to see him move the ball."

I laughed. "It's funny. The other way is okay, too, but I can't do it like he can."

"That's okay." Maybe if I tried really hard, I could move it like Dad, and this guy would stop being upset. I stared at the ball, but nothing happened. "It's okay," he repeated. "Sometimes you figure it out when you're older."

"Mom said since she's mundane, I'll just be boring like her."

His face did a weird thing, annoyed and sad and mad all at the same time, but it only lasted like a second before he was giving me that sad smile again. "Well, that's not always the case. Some very smart people have learned sometimes, you have special ways of doing tricks you can't see with your eyes, and it's not always because of which parent can do tricks."

I wiggled my toes on the weird carpet. The smell wasn't so bad now, but it made my nose itch, and I really wanted to go back to the other room and make sure Dad was getting up soon. "I can't do cool tricks like Dad, but Mom said I'm really good at learning things and being nice to people, and that's really important because sometimes people are mean and don't like boring people like us."

The man looked a little sadder, but he didn't have time to hide again. My mom opened the door. Her face was pale like when she got angry, and her makeup was all smoodgy. "What the hell, Jim?"

"Mom! Cuss word!"

She scooped me up, grabbing my Spider-Man light up shoes and setting me down on the squeaky sofa. After shoving my feet into the shoes, she turned around to face that guy. Jim. "You're not gonna answer me? No!" She poked her finger at him when he stood and tried to step closer. "No! Fuck you, Jim! I told you—Charlie told you—not Orrin. Not. Orrin."

Hearing Mom say the really bad word and sound so mad was scary. I started crying, and that thing inside me moved so fast, making it hard to breathe. I wanted Dad. I'd wanted him for days, and no one would tell me why I couldn't have him, and now he was sleeping and looking wrong, and Mom was using rude words. I couldn't breathe, and that made me cry harder.

She grabbed the ball and threw it hard at Jim. "Eloise," he said, his face red and splotchy like he had cried. "Don't do this."

"Stay away from Orrin. Stay away from me. It's bad enough Charlie is dead because of this bullshit and—"

"Mom?"

I knew that word because the same thing happened to Mom's mom last year, and I had to stay with Aunt Laura at her apartment. I got to play Mario with my cousin Dana, but I think Dana let me win because she's super good at Mario and usually never loses. And Royce couldn't spend the night when Grandma Becca died because Mom was so sad and had to go out of town with Dad, so we had to wait and have our sleepover later. But when dead happened to Grandma Becca, it meant she didn't come back. We didn't get to see her at Thanksgiving because Mom had to help Uncle David sell her house, and Grandma was never returning.

"Mom..." I was shaking. That thing inside me was growing big, so big I couldn't stop it from moving and hurting me. "Dad isn't like Grandma Becca. He's just wrong. But he can be okay. Get him out of that stupid bed. The bed is what's the matter." Even as the thought popped into my head, I decided that must be the problem. "Take him out of it, and he'll be okay. And we can go home. This place smells bad, and I want Dad back. He's been gone since Sunday, Mom!"

Mom made a bad sound, like she was hurt, and she squeezed me too hard, so I hurt too. "Orrin," she said in a weird voice. "Baby..."

"Eloise." Jim was very close to us now, and I didn't like it. He made Mom say Dad was dead, and that was a bad thing. "I know this is a nightmare, but when you're ready...when he's ready...I'm here."

"Fuck you." She squeezed me again. "I can't be here. I can't. I need to get Orrin out of here. You're all fucking ghouls!"

One of the guys who wore the suits at this place and told Mom about the Eternal Rest bed opened the door. "Is there something I can help with?" he asked in this soft whispery voice.

"Get everyone out," Mom said like a snarling dog. "Get them out *now*. They don't deserve to say goodbye to him!"

I shook hard, so hard I wanted to throw up. Goodbye meant dead, and dead meant Dad was staying in that stupid bed forever. I twisted and screamed, kicking Mom until she dropped me. I landed on my butt, then got on my feet too fast for her to grab me again. I ran hard as I could and bumped into some people, but I didn't care. They were all wrong, and I hated them.

Dad wasn't dead. Dad was wrong but not dead.

Mom grabbed me before I could get to Dad again. It hurt to breathe, and I couldn't hear anything but Mom crying and how my breath sounded funny.

Dad still didn't get up.

Chapter One

DREW

"I know I said you should get yourself a little something for your birthday, but this is a bit outré, isn't it? Since when did they start selling twinks on Amazon?"

With Ivan leaning over my shoulder, it was too late to click out of the screen. I kicked myself for not noticing his approach—his tendency to marinate in Spicebomb typically served as an advance guard. "He's under consideration for the position—"

"I'll bet." The bro-slap to my shoulder was just the icing on the cake. Ivan moved around my desk to park himself in the guest chair, legs sprawled in front of him and feet pushing my wastebasket to tilt at a precarious angle against the desk leg.

"*On the project*, Ivan." Calling him *dingus* was a near thing, but as Ivan was the CEO's son and nepotism was real, I exercised an iota of self-control. "Orrin applied for the biometric statistical analysis position, but Doctor DuMarque shunted his résumé over to the project because he thinks Orrin might be a good fit."

Ivan's brows shot up so fast, I was surprised they didn't achieve escape velocity. "Orrin Grimm?"

"Uh, yeah? You literally just saw his picture." I glanced back at the screen as if to check, but I didn't need to see his name again. Not only was it uncommon, it suited him. It sounded like a kind of geeky, quirky person, and, judging by his picture, it fit. He may have thought that fandom t-shirt under the white button-up was not noticeable, but I could totally make out Captain America's well-toned backside on the caricature emblazoned across Orrin's chest. "He apparently interviewed quite well for the position in biometrics, but DuMarque was insistent." I shrugged as if I couldn't care less, like I didn't have a tiny little aesthetic crush on Orrin Grimm already and hadn't had inappropriate-for-work thoughts about him the handful of times we'd had to interact on projects over the past few years. "I put him in the group to consider, if he's interested."

Ivan's expression went from amused and bored to shuttered and studiously neutral. "Whether or not he's interested, he needs to be moved to the team. You haven't spoken with him about this yet?"

I shook my head. Ivan's sudden, poorly hidden enthusiasm for Orrin was unsettling and set off a few alarm bells. "What's the big deal? I mean, his bona fides are good, but we have six others in the group. He being headhunted by Halloran and Reynard or something?"

What are you doing, Drew? Shut up. You want to see this guy in person, don't you?

Ivan's smile was slow and uneasy. "Or something." He rocked forward, bringing his legs together and swinging around to face me fully. "I've known Orrin for a while. Trust me when I say you *really* want him." He paused. "On the team, I mean."

His smirk was punchable.

"HICKS!"

I winced, hoping DuMarque didn't catch it in the reflection off the glass-fronted museum cases lining the wall across from me. The employee exit was so close. I could smell freedom. Well, as much freedom as I could wrangle from a lunch with my sister and her fiancé.

"Doctor DuMarque," I said, turning to face him with my work smile firmly in place. "I was just heading to meet my sister."

"This will only take a moment." Putting his arm around my shoulder, he led me further into the lobby museum, an homage to the history of magic and the attempts to revive the fading trait. "I wanted to speak with you about Orrin Grimm."

My face felt uncomfortably warm. I hoped DuMarque either couldn't see my blush or wrote it off to the gust of uncomfortably warm air from the HVAC system. Not the fact Orrin Grimm occupied way too much space in my brain already, and hearing his name made me feel like a teenager with a crush. DuMarque was a large man, what my grandmother would have called sturdy, leonine with a mane of shaggy, fading blond hair and piercing, dark eyes that made you feel hunted when he turned them—*really* turned them—on you.

Just like he was doing to me at that moment.

"Yes, sir. Based on my own, albeit limited, experiences with him and from what I saw on his CV and performance file, I think he'll be an excellent addition to the interview pool."

Excellent addition to the... *Christ, what the Hell is wrong with me?*

"Ah. I think you misunderstood when I sent you his information this morning. Hicks. There's no interview pool. Not anymore. I've dismissed the others. Grimm will be your direct subordinate for this department. In fact, y'all are the entire department for the time being." He gave me a weird sideways squeeze-shake thing, awkward as balls.

"I'm sorry, what?"

DuMarque raised one of his shaggy brows. "What part did you not understand?"

All of it. "What about the rest of the interviewees? What about protocol? What about—"

"Good God, Hicks," he laughed, his voice echoing off the display cases. "It's not like we're taking the rest of the potentials out back and shooting them. They're all internal applicants. They keep their positions. But Grimm is remarkably well suited for the position, and I think the pair of you will work well together." He hesitated, then led me over to one display, a long timeline running the length of one wall with a low case beneath it. Small holograms showed significant points in the history of known magic, up till about five years ago, when the space ran out of wall. "Grimm's parents were actually members of our very first cohort. Did you know?"

A cluster of people, about the size of my hand, huddled together in the display case, the faint blue-gray tinge of holographic projection making them look sickly. I recognized DuMarque, but not the four younger people standing in a cluster around him. Wait, no—one of the men looked quite a lot like Orrin, save for the nose, which was retroussé, where Orrin's was more of a sharp beak. Though I realized the young woman with her arms around the man's middle did have that familiar nose and the same tip-tilted smile I'd seen on Orrin from time to time.

"Charlie Grimm and Eloise Harper were college sweethearts, both from families with magical lines growing weaker over the past several generations. Coming from historically magical families, they were eager to revive the lines in the hopes they would pass on some of the gifts to their children one day." Smiling, he tapped the display glass as Charlie Grimm turned his head and said something to someone just out of range of the original camera's reach. The speakers were off, so I couldn't hear their voices, but I imagined he might sound like Orrin, the dry lilt and barely suppressed snark coloring his voice the handful of times I'd heard him speak. "They ended up working in the lab, Eloise as one of the techs and Charlie as our first dedicated data analyst. He's responsible for a lot of the basic infrastructure in the department, in fact.

"He died about twenty years ago, though, and Eloise was inconsolable. She refused to set foot in the lab again, refused to let Orrin get tested when he was twelve, even. She said..." He paused, looking up at the ceiling thoughtfully, like the words were hidden in the acoustic tiles. "She said she didn't want Orrin to suffer like his father. Eloise always felt Charlie worked himself to death," DuMarque said in a more confidential tone. "Still, it's in the blood because Orrin applied to work here straight out of college. He's truly remarkable. So much like his father. A genuine talent for what he does."

Hearing about Orrin's family was discomfiting. It felt too personal, too soon. But they were literally on display in the museum. And if they were members of the first cohort, they weren't exactly unknown, though the cohort members were all assigned a number and letter to show which cohort they belonged to. In the first? You would be subject 1A. Second? 1B. By the time they hired me, the lab had been up to W.

"It's not some misplaced sense of guilt or grief." DuMarque led me away from the hologram and toward the employee exit. "I want him in on this project because he *is* good at what he does. The best I've seen in decades. He has a real talent for it; if I didn't know better, I'd swear it was magic." He chuckled. "And his way with people is just unparalleled, really. Between the pair of you, you'll be brilliant at this project, and that's what we need right now."

I nodded slowly, letting him push the door open for me. "And what exactly *is* it we'll be doing?"

"Same thing you're doing now, but on a larger scale." He braced the door open, letting in the surprisingly cool for Houston autumn air, which thankfully smelled like fresh-cut grass with a tinge of pine needles and not like exhaust and creosote for once. "We've made amazing strides in the past few years with the Revive program, but there's been more than a handful of reports of magic appearing in lines dormant for over a century or in scientifically impossible ways. A manipulator producing a telepath, for example. Instead of relying on self-reporting, as we've been doing, the board has concluded it is imperative we track down the instances and determine if this is real, and, if it is, how it is happening.

"There have been concerns regarding possible industrial espionage," he added in a slightly lower tone, finally realizing we were standing half in and half out of the building, on a public sidewalk. "At the moment, nothing concrete, but we're hoping to determine whether these cases are purely urban legend or if the result of some sort of fundamental change in our understanding of magic and how the Revive program might be affected, especially if this is due to something underhanded."

"So we're...traveling?"

DuMarque shrugged. "Well, yes. Research has found people are more likely to give truthful answers in comfortable environments. Rather than forcing subjects to come all the way to our lab, we're going to them. Or, rather, you are." Flashing me another grin, he patted his coat pocket. "Ah, shit, I have to get going; I have a call with the Department of Human Developmental Research in ten minutes." He sighed, finally pulling his phone out. "Enjoy your lunch, Hicks. Oh, and do you have any plans for this weekend? We had to schedule a handful of Houston-area subjects for Saturday due to their work hours, so I want you and Grimm to give it a spin together, okay?"

I nodded, but he had already turned away, striding back into the darker parts of the building.

The way the metal door slammed and locked me out automatically felt more ominous than I would have liked.

Chapter Two

ORRIN

"It was entirely too many dicks, Orrin."

"No such thing!"

"Seriously," Royce insisted as he pulled his phone out of his messenger bag and began scrolling through pictures. "Imagine the perfect number of dicks in any situation. Then, like, multiply it by too many." He turned his phone to face me.

"Oh. Oh, yeah. That is...wow. I think one in the middle is staring at me." I leaned to one side, then slowly swayed the other way. "It's following me with its one eye."

"Thank you!" He shoved his phone back in his bag before taking a savage bite of his salad wrap. "I told Missy I would quit if she didn't stop assigning me the terrible exhibits."

"That was a plethora of peckers."

He nodded. "A cornucopia of cocks."

"A veritable deluge of dongs."

He snorted. "An enduring preponderance of pricks."

"A superfluity of schlongs."

"A torrent of tallywhackers, if you will."

"I most certainly will not!"

He tossed his crumpled sandwich wrapper at me. "That's not what I heard."

"Why are you still working for the gallery, anyway?" I grabbed the trash and lobbed it toward the wire can by the counter, missing by a wide margin and grimacing as I darted over to pick it up before returning to my seat. "I thought they offered you that assistant manager position at Harkin and Bates."

Royce worked for a chi-chi art gallery that sounded like a law firm running ads on daytime TV and specializing in personal injury suits. Missy, his boss, had beaten Royce by a very narrow margin—and a very blackmail-worthy video of their boss at the gallery accepting sexual favors for placement of artwork—for a promotion to gallery manager. She loved to ensure Royce got the worst jobs to handle.

We'd formed an informal lunch bitching session over our respective craptacular job situations. He had to deal with gallery showings for dilettantes who thought gigantic piles of dildos were a commentary on... something, I was sure. I was forced to go through spreadsheet after spreadsheet of data, making sure each little cell was filled in and then filing actual freaking paper copies of the same spreadsheets, like we were living in 1987 or something.

"It'd be a lateral move," he sighed. "I'd be doing the same damn thing for the same amount of money."

"No Missy, though," I pointed out.

"There's always a Missy."

I saluted him with a salt and vinegar chip.

"So enough about me," he finally sighed. "How goes everything with Sex on Legs?"

It was my turn to groan. "Fine. It's all fine. Super great. Awesome."

"Still being all morally upright and responsible and not throwing yourself naked on his desk after hours?"

I flicked another chip at him. "He's not even in my department."

"And if he was, you'd totally be doing the whole *I think I need help with my filing, Mr. Hicks. I'm looking for something starting with a D and ending with an O.*"

"Seriously?"

Royce wiggled his brows at me before his face slipped into more serious lines, leaning against the table. "I know you feel like you owe your dad this job," he said quietly. "But he wouldn't want you to do something you hate, and he definitely wouldn't want you to shut yourself off from the world because of one shitty experience."

I shook my head, my eyes hot and tight. If I opened my mouth, I'd make an awful sound instead of a word. He wasn't entirely wrong. I did feel a bit like I owed it to both of my parents to stay at HEEL, even if the job sucked. *Roots will protect you* had been one of my father's go-to aphorisms, something that made no sense to me when I was little. But as I got older, watching my mom bust her ass to make sure I was cared for, knowing she had to pull all kinds of strings and swallow pride and rage to finagle an interview for me at HEEL... I understood his words better. He—they—both wanted to be sure I succeeded in life, even if my success wasn't of the magic variety. If I quit HEEL, it'd be like throwing all of his, and Mom's, sacrifices back in their faces.

Royce reached for my hand, linking our fingers together and squeezing. "You deserve to live a little. Even just one date with the office hottie to break your self-imposed anchorism."

My sniffle was wet and kind of gross, to be honest. "Anchorites are super Catholic. I'm super not."

He patted my hand, withdrawing to pick at the remains of his lunch basket. "It's an analogy. Or a metaphor. One of those, I don't know. My degree's in art, not creative writing. But my point still stands: Take a chance, Ori. Live."

"You're like Teeny with a chew bone."

"Grrrrr," he agreed around a mouthful of lettuce wrap, which was actually pretty close to what my mom's Rottweiler sounded like.

"Even if it wasn't against workplace regulations," I had no idea if it was, but the whole *carrying on with a coworker* thing totally seemed like it would be, "he's all *unf,* and I'm *meh*. He's Midtown, and I'm Warehouse District." I wasn't sure if Office Hottie lived in Midtown, but he definitely had that vibe. I'd bet his place was all glass and shiny white walls and expensive furniture, amazing to get bent over... I squashed that thought with a quickness. A raging boner during lunch with Royce would only lead to him suggesting we get corn dogs for the next month.

We ate in silence for a minute until the sound of laughter filtered from the kitchen and into the dining area of the small deli we'd picked since it was midway between both our offices. Royce didn't glance back at the counter, but he went still and very pink. "Ah." I poked at him with one of my fries. "It wasn't just convenience that led you here, huh? What's his name?"

"Shut up."

"Unusual name, but then again, I'm not one to talk. My name sounds like a brand of vacuum cleaner." I snatched one of his pickles. "Seriously, why do you order pickles, then never eat them?"

"Because you never order pickles, and you love them." He pushed the tiny plastic container of baby gherkins my way.

"I don't order them because I always eat the ones you leave on the side."

"This is like a shitty version of *Gift of the Magi.*"

I picked up the last pickle and brandished it between two fingers. "The real gift was the preserved baby cucumber we found along the way."

"You need help, Ori. A lot."

Another burst of laughter rang out, and this time, Royce glanced over his shoulder. A tall, freckled redhead came out from the kitchen area and went behind the counter, carrying a stack of paper food baskets with the deli's logo. He set the baskets down on the counter and froze, his gaze fixed on the only other person in the dining area, a petite blonde with her face buried in a book, furiously making notes on a tablet. Royce sighed, his expression openly longing but not for either of the people at the counter. I knew Royce like I knew myself: he was lonely, even if he wouldn't admit it out loud. The redhead and the blonde both glanced over at us, then at one another. The woman smiled at the employee, and he flushed deep pink, then ducked behind the counter and...just kind of stayed there.

"Are you okay?" the woman asked. No reply. She looked over at us, concern creasing her brow. "Is he okay?"

Royce fidgeted in his chair, half-rising to stand, then dropping back down, leaning forward, then back. "I think?"

The kitchen door swung open and closed.

"Um. I think he just duck-walked into the kitchen so we couldn't see him," I offered.

Sighing, she folded in on herself, closing her book and shutting off her tablet. She didn't leave, but the disappointment was clear in every line of her posture.

Groaning, Royce dropped his head down to the table. "I'm so upset for them I don't even care my face is resting on the bare Formica."

I slid one of my unused napkins under his cheek. "C'mon, dumpling, don't be sad. I can go talk to him if you want." It wasn't an offer I made for just anyone. In fact, I usually ran fast and far as soon as talk turned to objects of affection (or, in most cases, lust). Especially at work. Once people figured out I had a knack for matchmaking, they bugged the hell out of me about their crush or tried to get me to go to a club or party with them. Ostensibly to hang out, but that veneer was always so thin, I could see right through it. The fact I sometimes went anyway made me pathetisad, I knew, but even us weirdo losers needed to get out of the house sometimes.

I had no fucking clue how I did it, honestly. If I saw two (or three and, in one case, four—definitely an eye-opener) people together, I knew whether they'd work out. Historically, every match I'd helped make had lasted.

Except my own. Cue sad trombone noise.

Groaning again, Royce rolled his head to one side to stare at me with a gimlet eye. "Don't say a word about it. I know you know."

I held up my hands. "I'm not saying a thing. But if there's someone in particular you want me to talk to with you..." I let out a sigh of relief when he shook his head. "Sorry. I mean, I'd do it, but I'm glad you said no."

Royce heaved his own sigh, then sat up and dabbed at his face with the clean napkin. "You'd tell me if I had sauerkraut on my face, right?"

Subject dropped, then. Message received loud and clear.

"Totally. Unless you thought you could convince Missy you were a fresh art piece, a tableau vivant about the struggles of cultured vegetables and the modern American palate."

"You're a dork." As I gathered my coat and scarf, he scooped up his trash and stacked our trays together. We stepped out of the deli and into the cool afternoon, a brisk and somehow damp breeze skittering down the narrow side street between the old buildings in downtown Houston. I wasn't entirely sure, but I thought I glimpsed a quick flash of red hair as the counter guy peeked out of the kitchen when the bell over the door signaled our departure.

Determinedly staring straight ahead, Royce adjusted his own scarf and smoothed the lapels of his suit jacket. "I have the rest of the day to write copy for the pile of dicks in the Sommerson Atrium. Quick, what's something that means phallic yet elegant?"

"I can't remember his name, but there was this guy I met at Super Happy Fun Land a few weeks ago..."

"Ass."

"That's the next exhibit." I poked him in the ribs. "Have fun with your deluge of dongs. I'm..." I groaned. "Ugh. I'm going to file shit." *Putting my Master's to good use.* Mom was thrilled I'd taken a job at the lab where she used to work, but I was fairly certain it was a dose of favors called in and a sprinkling of nepotism more than my innate abilities with computers and my brilliance in biometric analysis.

"Stop, stop, I'm jealous," he deadpanned. "Call me after. I have stuff for tacos, and I don't want to binge on seasoned meat by myself."

I was already walking backwards, raising my hand in a goodbye. "There's another dick joke in there somewhere, I just know it."

His middle finger bid me farewell.

Laughing, I turned and hurried the rest of the way back to my office in the gleaming chrome-and-glass cube that was the HEEL research facility and the six-inch thick pile of spreadsheets I had to enter manually, thanks to the security measures the new department lead had put into place. I had a solid ten minutes before I needed to be back at my desk, and I fully intended to spend every one of them dicking around and avoiding anything even remotely involving responsibility.

MY LUCK WAS BOUND TO run out sooner rather than later. I'd avoided DuMarque all of Thursday afternoon, even though it meant I had to skedaddle out the side entrance onto McHenry Street. I would miss the bus I usually took from the stop in front of the building, which was officially two blocks away from the side entrance, but it was fine. Walking was good for me, or so I'd been told. In fact, I did a lot of it on Friday morning when I heard DuMarque was lurking on the sixth floor before his weekly call-in with the lab managers and the research teams in Europe, Asia, and Africa.

It was sixty-seven steps from my cubbyhole office to the old elevator that shook and rattled to the first floor. Then forty steps to the little courtyard with the broken fountain, an unintentional homage to Brutalism. Thirty-six steps around the fountain for one lap. Then, from there, reverse it back to the elevator door, but take a pit stop at the old vending machine with the Plexiglass viewing window and faux-woodgrain paneling, mainly because it sold TAB and Fresca unironically. Once upstairs, I had to walk thirty-two steps past the open door and the interoffice window (seriously, why did they put windows *inside* offices?) of the Information and Recruitment Office. IRO. Or, as I called it in my head, *ruh-roh*. It wasn't dangerous because of anything exciting like experiments that might go haywire or even an aggressive fax machine—and yes, even at the Human Engineering and Enhancement Lab, we had fax machines. Nothing says *please, give us research funding and lots of grants* like tech from the mid-eighties.

No, IRO was dangerous because they'd caught on to my particular talent. Not a talent like the subjects of HEEL, with their increased physical abilities and, frankly, unfair good looks, but my ability to matchmake with a high degree of success. It seemed like every time anyone from IRO so much as thought I was walking past, they launched themselves out of their fancy ergonomic chairs and cornered me to ask about so-and-so down in QA or whether Doctor What's-Her-Face was single.

As I passed the Danger Zone, I sped up my steps, head down and determined to make it back to my office without being stopped now that it was after one p.m., when DuMarque had his weekly call.

"Orrin! Hey, Orrin!"

Shit. That's what I got for indulging in a moment of sadsack navel-gazing.

Ivan DuMarque, IRO receptionist and serial monogamist, spotted me walking past, and now I had to run for it. I ducked my head and walked faster, wishing I'd grabbed my phone out of my desk drawer before going on my fourth walk of the day. The only thing in my hand was an unopened can of soda, which meant I had two options: turn and lob it at Ivan, hoping it hit him somewhere nonlethal, or shake the can and open it, using the spray to obscure his vision and cause a distraction.

Oh. Wait. I could also just brazen it out and hope for the best. So three options, then. Especially since "just tell him to go away" wasn't a viable one. Ivan not only fielded the calls, emails, and visits for IRO—he was also the son of Doctor Calder DuMarque. Head of the biostatistics department and CEO of HEEL.

Because life liked to point in my face and laugh sometimes.

"Orrin! Wait up!" Ivan's long legs closed the distance between us, and he grabbed my shoulder. "Hey, I was hollering for you, dude. I have a quick question! You busy? Sorry, forgot who I was talking to." He laughed, giving me one of those bro-y shoulder thumps before slinging his arm across my back and pulling me in for an awkward, humid side-hug. Charming.

"I have the Fuller file to get through before the end of the day, so..." Fuller's file was easy but lengthy, the perfect excuse to spend at least two hours nowhere near DuMarque or anyone else needing the literal hookup.

He'd been registered as a participant in the first study, back in the eighties, and had been keeping up with his check-ins ever since. He was a regular the PR and IRO liked to trot out at recruitment and press events because he was so goddamn charming, the literal poster boy for the program. A former college athlete injured at the cusp of his professional baseball career, Fuller had been part of the initial cohort of test subjects for HEEL and HERO. He had been exposed to the HEEL tech, HERO (seriously... Human Enhancement Retrocellular Optimization, because somebody really wanted to have the acronym HERO involved in the damned project). Out of ten subjects, he'd been the most successful. The tech not only healed his torn ligaments and nerve damage but made him the ideal athlete—increasing his speed, strength, stamina, and endurance. I'm not sure how, but it even improved his curve ball.

Okay, that was probably down to the suddenly available top of their game trainers, exercise facilities, nutritionists, and everything else the comes with being a favored test subject for HEEL. But they liked to bring it up at the press junkets and thought it was hilarious.

But most importantly, the tech had sparked his magic back to life. They'd become known for their telekinetic abilities which, while not the wackadoodle stuff you see in movies, was impressive as fuck and important over the centuries.

Lucky bastard.

People loved to cite magic's use during different wars or to force political hands, and lines like Fuller's family had often been exploited (I'm sorry, "chosen") by governments who saw the threat potential in telekinetics at their disposal. But people like my father's family were known for their contributions to the arts, to literature and creative pursuits. With quite a bit of foot-dragging, HEEL finally accepted all of the major lines into their program, not just the ones like Fuller, but I often wondered how hard they fought to make the tech work for people who wouldn't manifest the showy abilities.

"It can wait," Ivan chided. "This is important." He leaned in, wrapping his fingers just above my elbow a little *too* tightly. (Though, honestly, was there such a thing as the perfect grasp when someone was grabbing hold of you without your permission? That can of soda in my hand was looking more and more like an improvised ranged weapon.) "My father wants to see you in the lab. ASAP." He gave my arm a tug and me a smirk.

"Why didn't he just page me?" Not on an actual pager, thank the powers that be. They were super-dedicated to old office tech here (see: fax machine: use of, and file boxes full of floppy disks: things I have to file and dust) but our "pagers" were just fancy watches looped in to an interoffice communications system. If someone needed one of us somewhere, we'd get a buzz, and the location would show on the tiny screen.

We were supposed to be able to track our steps on them, but I'd turned that shit off. It was one thing for my boss to buzz me when they needed something but another for them to track how often I had to use the john. Or took aimless walks around the facility. So far no one had mentioned the gaps in my biometric data in the system, but since I was below the lowest rung on the ladder at HEEL, I didn't think anyone really cared.

Ivan shrugged, already tugging me toward the end of the hall where a single, smudged elevator door waited. "He didn't give me details, just said to grab you if I saw you."

"I doubt he meant literally."

Ivan's laugh was loud and annoying. "You're funny. Does anyone ever tell you that? You're hilarious, Orrin." He gave my arm a squeeze and shake. "Funny *and* interesting! Killer combo, huh?"

Okay. Even for Ivan, this was weird. He'd flirted with me (or rather, *at* me), tried to sweet-talk his way into my good graces so I would "help him out, man" with this nurse or that tech, but he'd never been so...over the top hey-buddy-hey-pal with me. It definitely set some alarms blaring in my brain. "What's going on, Ivan? If this is about Jameson—"

"Hm? Oh, no, it's not about Jameson. He's super happy with that site services chick you set him up with." While we waited for the elevator doors to wheeze open, he rolled his eyes. "They're disgusting together. I'm glad you helped me dodge that bullet, man. Jameson is way into the whole white-picket-fence shebang, and that is just possibly the worst outcome for a relationship."

"Um."

As we waited for the elevator, he kept chattering, even as he used his own pass card to activate the button panel inside the carriage and access the lab floor. I tried to tune out Ivan while we shuddered and lurched downward. The staff elevators sucked, as outdated as the rest of the actual working part of the HEEL facilities, not at all shiny and sleek like the public-facing part, with desk chairs that didn't wobble ominously if you coughed. We lurched to a jarring halt, making my teeth clack and Ivan sway against me.

"Sorry." He grinned, letting go of my arm to sling his own over my shoulder and do that annoying buddy shoulder-shake maneuver. "Come on, Dad's been champing at the bit to talk to you all morning."

"Then why didn't he just page me?" I wiggled out from under Ivan's arm. The door slid open to reveal the small, gray alcove where we needed to stand and wait for our scans before stepping into the next part of the security protocol.

Ivan flashed me another of his too-gummy smiles. Seriously, why did the man have so much gum showing when he smiled? Was it a dental issue? "He knew I'd be seeing you."

There went the bro arm again.

I twisted away as the scan finished. The painless and invisible beams took in our vitals and the tiny little significant details making us discernible from one another to the biometric readers. Like an airlock, the doors hissed open, and we stepped into a slightly larger room, this one manned by two guards with metal detector wands and a complex ventilation system capable of detecting chemical residue indicating explosives or even certain toxic substances to drug the researchers in some baroque heist attempt.

I sincerely thought whoever designed the lab's security system was a mix between Wile E. Coyote Super Genius, Q from James Bond, and also deeply paranoid. We were wanded, sniffed by the ventilation system, and then passed through to yet another antechamber. This one had plain old desk guards waiting to check our ID cards and do a quick retinal scan with a handheld device. Deeming us safe, they sent us on to the last stop.

"Hey," Ivan called cheerily as we stepped out of the checkpoint and into the front office for the lab. "Dad around?"

"Dad? Well, the man *I* call Dad is in Cheyenne, Wyoming, so the answer to your question is no," Sharon, the lab's receptionist and one of the longest-running employees of HEEL, said with a smile so sharp it could probably perform surgery. "If you mean Doctor DuMarque, he's in, but he's with a guest at the moment. Have a seat." She flicked her glance to me, and her smile dimmed. "I'll get you some tea."

"I'm fine." Waving her off, Ivan manhandled me over to one of the guest chairs. "We need to see my...Doctor DuMarque."

"Your Doctor DuMarque will be out in a minute." Sharon swept a gimlet-eyed glance over me. "What're you doing down here anyway, Grimm? I'm still waiting for the Fuller file."

I rolled my eyes. "I told Ivan I had to finish it," I sighed, angling for a bit of low-rung-on-the-corporate-ladder commiseration, but Sharon just sniffed at me again and resumed whatever she'd been doing on her desktop computer.

"Okay, listen. Dad's talking with the guy from the Violations team."

"Shit." The Violations team was some crappy business. The HEEL program wasn't exactly under governmental control, but it was *very keenly observed*, as the higher-ups liked to say. The military and other groups could potentially use the things done in the lab. *Other groups* were our allies or factions we wanted to kiss ass with by offering them a really nice gift—enhanced humans.

The thing was...so far, no one had developed the ability to manifest things out of thin air, super strength, or anything the government-issued boffins liked to play with. Instead, we had people like Fuller, who was a stellar athlete before taking part in the first gen experiments and only became better afterward. However, HEEL's own in-house monitoring department zealously guarded everyone who had taken part in any experimental cohort.

So...yeah, nothing weird at all, right?

Ivan had gotten super into his fidgeting, which consisted mostly of finger-combing his hair and muttering to me to "just follow my lead, okay?" on a loop, by the time the door to Doctor DuMarque's office opened and the man himself stuck his head out. "There you both are. Come on, then. Let's get this done with so I can get to lunch."

Ivan popped up so fast I was surprised he didn't get a nosebleed. Hooking my elbow, he tugged me to my feet, half-dragging me toward his father's office before I could get my legs under myself. "Here we are," Ivan chirped, all but shoving me into the office.

"Hey!" Jerking free, I retained the tiniest shred of dignity by stepping out of Ivan's reach and turning to face Doctor DuMarque. "Ivan says you were looking for me?"

Okay. Maybe not so much dignity as "stating the obvious."

Doctor DuMarque flapped a hand toward the two chairs across from his desk. "Please, sit. This won't take long. I told Ivan I'd page you, but he insisted on getting you himself." He didn't really roll his eyes so much as glance upward toward the ceiling, but I grokked. I made that face fairly often during the workday.

"It was no trouble," Ivan said. Damn near singsonged, really. He was laying it on thick, whatever "it" was. I'd thought maybe he had been angling for my help with someone he had his eye on, but, unless he'd taken a hard turn for the ick, the only person in the office was his dad, and Ivan definitely wasn't trying to get all Greek tragedy with him.

Doctor DuMarque shot his son a quelling glare before turning his smile on me. "I understand you've asked to be considered for the biostatistics position down here in the lab."

He damn well knew that was the case; he was the one in charge of the program. But I smiled and nodded. "Yes, it's part of my five-year plan."

Yeah, I know. I hated myself for saying it. But those buzzwords really caught the ear of HR and the higher-ups, who loved to throw around words like *synergy* and talk about "dovetailing and facilitating" projects and plans.

Nodding thoughtfully, DuMarque reached for a stack of file folders on his desk. "Well, I don't know if Ivan's caught you up to speed on what's going on, but that position has been culled from the lab."

I'm pretty sure I kept my shriek of outrage internal. "Oh?"

He gave me a sympathetic wince. "I know you were working toward it, and, frankly, if it had been entirely up to me, I'd have had your name at the top of the list."

There was a very pregnant pause. I was supposed to say something, but I couldn't think of what. I *wanted* to say a few things that would get me fired, no doubt, and even in my fit of internal pique, I knew would sound whiny and downright douchey if I said them aloud. Instead, I forced a tiny, sick smile and nodded. Beside me, Ivan made an impatient noise. If an eye roll had a sound, that was it.

The quiet had stretched out too long and was in danger of getting a cramp before DuMarque finally spoke again. "Well, I know it's not your, ah, dream job here at HEEL, but I do want to make you an offer. We have a new position opening soon. An entire department, actually. Within days, in fact, and I think you'd be a perfect fit. It involves not only the unique skills you possess in biostatistical analysis but a certain level of ability with software engineering." He paused, giving me one of *those* looks that always means *I know the answer already, but I'm giving you the chance to fuck up by lying to me.* "You minored in computer science, didn't you? With a focus on software engineering?"

Ugh... My good decisions about what minor would benefit my career were coming back to bite me in the ass. "Yes, sir. I actually considered a double major, but I would have had to stay another three semesters to take three more classes."

DuMarque made one of those dad noises, a humming and thoughtful "that's nice, son" sound. "Well, I don't have to tell you about the program's history or what getting a fresh influx of funding to develop tech and further investigate the possibilities of HERO's experiments means for the lab. As it is, we have fifty humans out in the world with enhancements and..." He trailed off, looking awkward. "Well. There's been some further developments, thanks to the recent revival of the HERO project. We're opening an Enhanced Humans Management Office, and I feel you would be the perfect fit for the position of head investigator."

Ivan couldn't take it anymore. "I've been promoted to project lead for this one!"

"Hell of a jump, from receptionist to project lead," I said. *Shit...*

I glanced at DuMarque, but he had a faint smirk on his lips. *Dodged that one...*

Ivan scowled. "I have experience as a project manager, Orrin."

I bit down hard on my tongue, sending a sharp spike of pain through my thoughts and silencing the—frankly rude—snark I was dying to spit out.

"I've organized the winter holiday cookie exchange for five years now," Ivan continued. "And the company lacrosse league."

"We have a lacrosse league?"

Ivan waved me off. "You'd hate it. There's sweating."

"Fair." I nodded.

"*Anyway,*" DuMarque said just a tiny bit loudly, "while I know this isn't the position you'd had your heart set on, I feel you would be a perfect fit and really help the lab reach our goal here." He shot Ivan a glance that made him settle back in his chair, and I swear that man was pouting at his own father. "We're going through the data from the first three cohorts back in the eighties and early nineties. When we compare the data we initially gathered to more recent visits to the facilities, we've been finding some discrepancies."

Oh, shit...I knew where this was going. I was about to get a promotion from glorified data entry clerk to glorified data entry clerk with a slightly bigger office. Still, I smiled and nodded. "So, you're looking for someone to help go through the old files to parse out the errors?"

"That's the thing," DuMarque sighed. "There are no errors in the collections. It was very straightforward stuff, hard to fuck up, really. But recent collections on surviving members from the original cohorts have shown a distinct change over time, indicating possible propagation. Lately, the incidence of non-program enhanced humans has spiked in reports, becoming worrisome enough for HEEL to launch an investigation."

Everything took a moment to click. "Wait, seriously?"

Ivan huffed. "No, this is all an elaborate ruse. I really dragged you up here to find out if I had a chance with Sharon."

"Not if it was gold-plated and shot out chocolate," Sharon called from the front office.

DuMarque cleared his throat. "As I was saying, the current situation is potentially a detriment to the future of HEEL and HERO. Lines of magic reemerging without a traceable link back to the lab looks bad for us, frankly."

I frowned, the little hamster on the wheel in my brain starting to jog rather than keep to the usual ambling pace. "Isn't that a good thing, though? If magic is returning—"

"It's not a good thing," Ivan said before his father could reply. "The abilities appearing aren't following the lineages they belong to. A Touch family line gaining the ability to Know, for example." He shook his head.

For once, I was with Ivan on something. "A touch-based telepath suddenly being able to use limited future-sight would be unheard of," I murmured. "That'd be like a lion giving birth to an elephant or something."

DuMarque stepped in smoothly. "While it may seem, on the surface, to be positive, there has been no recorded instance of a non-magical person manifesting abilities without a testing error in early childhood. And since the development of rapid serum testing for genetic markers indicative of magical ability..." He smiled a self-satisfied smirk. HEEL had developed the most widely used, most accurate test. "Investors are speculating test subjects have had access to rogue tech, possibly created by competitors."

Halloran. I didn't say his name out loud, but I didn't have to. Ivan wrinkled his nose and practically spat, "I still say you should sue for intellectual theft or corporate espionage or—"

"Or," DuMarque raised his voice just a slight bit, enough to silence Ivan. "Or we investigate the matter and determine whether or not the leaks occurred via our lab first. And ensure we have an airtight case, and nothing can be blamed on HEEL or the HERO program. If, *if*, we pursue action against another party, we want to be sure there is no way it can be turned back on us." A small smile creasing his cheeks, his silver-dark gaze shifted to me. "We don't like nasty surprises here."

The hiss-pop of the lab door opening made all three of us jump. DuMarque recovered first, his plastic grin in place as he held out one arm, game-show-host style. "Hicks! Come in! Come in! I thought you were out for the rest of the day!"

My heart did this funny swoop and lurch straight down to my pants and right back up again.

"Sorry, the meeting with, er, the client got canceled." Andrew Hicks stepped into the lab like I'd summoned him from that dirty fantasy I'd had at lunch. Light blue button-up with the sleeves rolled up showing his forearms, that faint stubble he never seemed able to get rid of, those *glasses*... "You okay?" His brows drew down.

All three men were staring at me. "Oh. Sorry. Just had a thought."

"Don't hurt yourself," Ivan quipped. "Andrew here is going to be joining our team."Andrew smiled again, this time a little smaller as his gaze darted between DuMarque and Ivan. "Please, call me Drew. And leading it, I thought?"

DuMarque nodded, waving one hand airily. "You're team lead, yes, yes, but most importantly, you are going to be working directly with the lab's hidden gem, Orrin Grimm. He's the best biostatistical analyst I've ever met, after his own father."

Was I? That was news to me. "Um, thank you? I didn't know his work was still—"

DuMarque kept talking, cutting me off. As he rattled on, my face heated under the sudden, sympathetic glance from Drew. "And since this project is make or break, you'll be starting immediately. Orrin, I hope you don't mind coming in on Saturday to get the first round of interviews in."

What the hell was it with these people and their bro-slaps?

"I, um...I actually had a few things scheduled," I began, but DuMarque's crimped frown made me trail off in a sigh. "What time?"

Drew fidgeted under DuMarque's questioning gaze. "Er, is nine alright? It looks like it should only be an hour or so."

"Make it eight," DuMarque declared. "And you'll be here half the day. Son," he added, and I winced when Ivan preened, only to wilt when his father turned his attention on me, "your father really would be proud. He gave all he had to our research, and knowing you're doing the same..." He sighed. "Well. He'd definitely think you're following in his footsteps." He gave us all one of those officious nods corporate drones of a certain age got issued by HR and strode from the lab, leaving the three of us staring at one another awkwardly.

"Looks like it's your lucky day." Ivan bared his teeth in a rictus grin. I thought he might be talking to Drew, but I couldn't help but think maybe, for me, it was.

Chapter Three

DREW

"Still working at the freak factory?"

"Christ, Vick!"

My sister Dee, bless her heart, could only sink so far in her chair. Her nearly full-term pregnancy bump kept her from being able to slide all the way under the table in the middle of Christophero's, which was really too fancy a restaurant for the fight I could feel coming on.

I knew we should've gone to Waffle House.

Victor Hayden, her fiancé and father of her unborn child, flashed that famous toothy grin at me and leaned across the table. "Seriously, though," Victor stage-whispered. "Why the Hell do you keep working there? I've told you I can get you on at the division in a heartbeat. Someone with your skills?" He let out a low whistle through those damn too-white teeth, leaning back in his chair with a shake of his head. "In. A. Heartbeat."

"I'm happy at the lab." I breathed a sigh of relief when I spotted our waiter heading over with a tray of drinks. Undoubtedly, Victor's presence meant something was getting comped. I just hoped it was the drinks, something that wasn't going to put a dent in the waitstaff's take for the day, and not our entire meal.

The few times I'd been out with my sister and her fiancé, Victor, they had made huge productions of effusive thanks for the generosity of whatever establishment we'd been at. And yet he blustered away without leaving so much as a penny for the waitstaff who had to deal with their complicated orders, trundling back and forth to the kitchen multiple times because the first time was never right.

"And, frankly, I don't need to justify my career to you, Vick. If that's the entire purpose of this little get-together, let me know so I can go ahead and leave, save us both the trouble."

Smiling with fixed expressions, Vick and Dee were both quiet. Our waiter set my glass of tea, Dee's lemon water, and Vick's whiskey down at our places, fussing with Vick's drink until Vick murmured, "Enough, son."

"I'll, um. I'll be back with your starters in a few minutes," he squeaked, darting back toward the kitchen.

Vick clicked his tongue softly. "I'm going to have a word with Rodrigo. He hires these kids who stutter and won't make eye contact. It's disrespectful. Next thing, I'll find out he's been hiring some freaks from your little science experiment."

Acid hatred bubbled up in my chest.

"What are we doing here?" I sighed. "Dee, if this is about your wedding—"

"It is!" She perked up, rummaging in her handbag to bring out the thickest, most bookmarked planner in existence. The first time she whipped it out, the fact she had a physical notebook of wedding plans instead of keeping everything on her tablet had surprised me, but I'd come to realize she loved the drama of flashing that glittery white cover, the porcupine spines of tabbed pages and furls of ribbons marking especially important sections. There was no mistaking her notebook for what it was. Combined with the absolute knuckle-knocker of a ring Victor had given her, it was guaranteed to draw appreciative and often envious sighs and coos from whoever she was trying to impress.

Today, I think that person was Victor, judging by the looks she kept darting him as she flipped through her book to a section marked with wide blue ribbon and a flutter of sticky notes. "I've finally decided on the groomsmen's colors," she announced grandly. "Cerulean and hydrangea."

"Blue and pink," I said, nodding.

I tried not to be an asshole. I really did. When Dee first started seeing Victor Hayden, I'd been unpleasantly surprised but figured it wasn't my business or my problem. Famous for his anti-magic stance, he had gone from local celebrity to internationally famous talk show host in just a few short months after staging an exposé on a group claiming to be a family of magicals. They had been scamming people, offering them hope and help regaining lost powers, when in fact they had been dosing them with hallucinogens and robbing them blind. It had been ridiculous and baroque, but it had lit a fire under the anti-magical groups, especially the louder ones, and Victor had become their messiah.

The fact my sister was marrying him was nauseating. The fact I was expected to be a groomsman? Well, also nauseating but in a different way. The first was like being seasick. The second was like riding a roller-coaster after eating every hot dog, cotton candy cone, and slushie in the amusement park, then getting stuck upside down.

I needed to demur before we got as far as a tuxedo fitting but...ugh. Dee was still my little sister, even when she made dumbass decisions.

"Cerulean and hydrangea are two very different shades than just blue and pink," she said tartly. "Victor loves them. Don't you?"

Victor smiled vaguely in her direction, his gaze fixed on the front door to the restaurant. "Blue's lovely. Matches your eyes, baby."

Dee smiled sweetly at him. "And you'll look amazing in that *cerulean* vest you chose, Vicky."

His smile soured. "It's a waistcoat. And if you insist on a nickname, it's Vick. Remember, *Dee*?"

Dee made a face. "Fine, fine. Oh!" She giggled, placing her hand on her belly. "She's really going bananas in there today!" She looked at me with a shadow of her old self in her eyes, the little sister who stuck to my side for years. The one who'd been my best friend since we were in elementary school together. "Want to feel your niece kicking?"

I reached across the table to press my fingers on the swell of her belly. A moment later, a soft thump bounced off the palm of my hand. "Oh my god! That's her?"

"Sure as hell ain't a gas bubble," Victor chortled, his voice carrying. "Though God knows she's been belching and farting like a champ since hitting the whale stage of pregnancy."

Dee colored, ducking her head and busying herself with her planner.

"Hey," I hissed sharply. "Maybe try not embarrassing her, huh?" Vick's eyes flared, and his lips thinned.

Here we go. I almost relished the idea of having it out with the asshole. Even without his notoriety and his bigoted fan club, he was terrible to my sister, and I dreaded how he would be with his own child.

"You know... " Vick pushed aside his drink and started to rise.

Saved by the waiter again. I made a mental promise to make sure I got a huge tip into his hands before leaving the restaurant, even if I had to go back to the kitchen and track him down to do it. "Um, fried avocado fingers," he slid a plate in front of Dee, "ceviche for you, sir," he deposited Vick's plate, "and shrimp tostada for you, sir."

The waiter left so fast, he may have had a contrail.

Dee picked at her food. "I'm not as hungry as I thought," she said, breaking the brittle quiet at our table. "Maybe I'll just stick to water." She sent Vick another *notice me* look. "Besides, I need to be careful. I don't want it to be too hard to get my figure back after she's born."

Vick grunted in agreement. "You've got an important job lined up, honey. Looking good on my arm." He flashed her a chiclet grin before turning a sharp, predatory gaze on me. "Did Dee tell you the good news?"

I took a bite of my food. As delicious as it was, it was going to sit poorly thanks to the company I was keeping. "Well, I already know about the baby, so I can only assume the good news is Dee's getting back into illustrating?" Before things with Vick got serious, my sister had been working on a series of graphic novels for elementary and middle school age groups, mostly science stuff, intended to make education more accessible to kids who might have trouble with regular text books or even just find them boring.

I don't know what Vick said to her or what transpired when I wasn't around, but she stopped doing it one day, stopped getting back in touch with her editors, stopped trying to make contact with schools and publishers. She changed her entire personality just to make Vick happy.

It was one of the very few things on earth making me envious of magicals. If I had even a tiny iota of any power, I'd find a way to break Vick's hold over Dee.

Vick snorted, popping a shrimp into his mouth and crunching. The ass didn't even bother to take off the tails! It was either the weirdest flex imaginable, or he had some bizarre tastes in food. "No, she's done with her coloring books for good. No, the good news is..." He glanced around, and I could feel it coming.

What was *it*? I didn't know. I just knew *it* was bad and barreling down at me like a runaway train on an icy track.

"I've decided to run for state Senate!"

I was right. My food was definitely not a good idea.

"YOU LOOK LIKE SHIT."

"Thank you. I feel like shit, too."

Mina, my best friend at work—well, outside of work, too—leaned on my desk and fixed me with one of her soon-to-be-patented mother hen glares. "And if you look like shit, and feel like shit, what are you supposed to do?"

"You're not my therapist, Mina."

If she rolled her big green eyes back any further, she'd get a cramp. "No, but I'm a good listener, and I'm not afraid to tell you when you need to get your head out of your ass. Or fuck off," she added after a thoughtful pause. "So, talk to me, and I'll tell you which one it is this time." She punctuated each word with a tap of her neat, short acrylic nail against the tip of my nose.

"I hate it when you do that."

"Yes, but I'm your bestie, so I can get away with it."

"That seems kind of...not good."

"And this seems kind of like avoidance." Mina slid to her feet and grabbed the guest chair from the corner of my office. It was not nearly as tiny as Orrin's, but it was no corner penthouse suite overlooking Memorial Park. Still, I had room for a small loveseat, a coffee table that seemed to collect a disturbing number of pamphlets from various corporate retreat facilities, and the chair Mina grabbed that squeaked like an angry mouse whenever anyone sat down.

Well, everyone but Mina. She always managed to sink gracefully into it, nary a high-pitched sound from her or the chair.

"Now. Talk."

I groaned, but gave in and told her the entire awful lunch story, right down to Vick's under-voiced warning to "watch my ass" and "don't fuck things up for Dee," and the loud, jocular, back-slapping farewells after a celebrity-struck manager comped our lunches. I managed to slip two twenties under the saltshaker before Vick boomed out that Dee needed to "get a wiggle on" and made some half-assed joke about how she waddled.

"And you let him live?" Mina's brows disappeared somewhere around her hairline. "Did you not have a knife on the table?"

"The man eats shrimp shells," I reminded her. "It's probably a sign that it'll take some sort of crustacean-based weapon to kill him."

She made a face. "I think maybe it's time to cut ties, darlin'. I know you love Dee," she rushed to say before I could protest, "but this whole thing with the asscanker future brother-in-law? It's only going to get worse."

"But—"

"But," she said firmly, "I'm not gonna strongarm you into doing it. However, I think it's something you need to give some serious consideration because his whole "running for state Senate" thing? Even if he doesn't make it far, it's gonna bring his family a *lot* of attention. And you need to think about how that attention is going to not only affect you personally, but professionally. Your sister..." She blew out a harsh breath. "Well. I barely know Dee. But you can be there for her without *being there* for her."

It wasn't as simple as Mina suggested, and we both knew it. But there was no time to argue the point; her desk phone shrilled. She had to get back to her own duties, leaving me to put my head down on my desk and hide from the world for another ten minutes.

THE BRIGHT SLIVER TO the afternoon came with an email from DuMarque. Travel plans for Orrin and me. Our first interview was to take place in Beaumont, Texas, which was not much of a drive from Houston (unless you counted the time spent sitting in traffic, which anyone from the area always knew to expect). That being said, the interviews were spaced out over the day, meaning we'd either get to claim about seven hours of overtime, or the lab could pony up for an inexpensive hotel for the night and save themselves some pocket change.

At the sight of the hotel reservations, I had a tiny flicker of excitement. I entertained a very brief fantasy of *oh no; they screwed up the rooms and there's only one left and it only has one bed, oh no* before I forced myself back to reality and sent confirmation of receipt back to DuMarque's secretary. Orrin had been cc'd on the email, so I didn't have an excuse to contact him and let him know the details.

Damn it.

I rattled off a few emails I actually *did* need to send, reserved the conference room for the Saturday interviews on site at the lab building, and made a note to text my sister later before I noticed I still had the employee information tab open on the lab intranet.

And Orrin was staring back at me from my screen with those bright blue eyes.

And I was possibly being a tiny bit obsessive.

Mina, in her office across from me, was frowning at her own computer. Glancing up, she shot me a grin before returning to whatever she was trying to untangle. She'd tell me I was being a creep. And she'd probably be right. I'd been not-so-subtly crushing on Orrin for a while, and our half-day on Saturday was going to be the first time we were actually paired up together for a project.

I had the distinct feeling it was a test run, and, if things went terribly, DuMarque had a back-up team ready to go.

With another glance at Orrin's steady, digital stare, I closed the intranet tab and forced myself to pay attention to the files I needed to sign off on. I absolutely did not spend any time trying to figure out which shirt I should wear the next day that would look good without making it clear I was *trying* to look good.

Chapter Four

ORRIN

"It sounds shady as fuck," Royce announced, tipping his bottle of beer at me in that sagely pontificating way he had when he rode that line between pleasantly buzzed and flat-out tipsy. "Like that bit at the end of *Raiders* where they're all like *top men, Doctor Jones,* and it's just a shitty storage unit next to a jar of someone's face."

I wrinkled my nose. "You're mixing up *Raiders* with *Silence of the Lambs.* That was the one with the face in a jar."

He waved his free hand airily. "My point stands. This is shady as fuck. Why are they trying to track down people? That sounds like some black ops type shit. And, no offense, my darling, but why do they want you involved? Isn't that like..." He made a face at some spot in the middle distance, taking a long pull from his Tecate before continuing. "Isn't that like entirely out of your wheelhouse? Why do they need a biometric analyst on this?"

That had been bugging me, too. I gave him the only answer I'd been able to come up with: "I'm cheaper than hiring out for someone actually experienced in tech, and they think I'll have some loyalty to the program because of Mom and Dad." I was also pretty sure they were hoping having my name—my father's name, by extension—attached to this new project would lend them some cachet with investors and oversight committees.

Royce made a small, sad sound. "I miss your dad." He tilted his head like he would rest it on my shoulder, then seemed to remember we were sitting across his little breakfast bar from one another, and he was more likely to face-plant into his guacamole than snuggle. Since he moved to my street at age two,, Royce and I had grown up together. He'd spent more nights in my room than his own, my parents used to joke. I didn't know at the time it was only partially because of our friendship, that his parents were having problems. All I knew was my best friend got to sleep over even on school nights sometimes, and my folks loved him like a second son.

"He's haunting me this week," I sighed. Between the hologram and hearing DuMarque praise him over and over and just the fact he was—is—my dad and I couldn't escape his face whenever I looked in the mirror, it seemed like he was everywhere.

"And I think he'd agree with you," I added before Royce could apologize for mentioning him, or I could get more maudlin. "It's weird, and I get a funky vibe off the entire thing, but I don't really have another choice. If I quit, I'd need to scramble and find another job before rent's due. If I refuse and say I don't want the new position..." I sighed and took the last sip of my own beer. "I'm pretty sure I'd get fired or something."

Royce peeled his label, dropping bits of the damp paper onto his empty plate. "Or you could, I dunno, see if Halloran and Reynard is hiring." He shot me a look from under lowered lashes. "Just to see if the market's good, you know?"

I groaned. "Royce..." Halloran and Reynard wasn't exactly a huge competitor in the field, but they were definitely a competitor. One of the few who functioned solely on private funding and eschewed grants tied up in pretty terms and conditions for use of the money. They were almost laughably small, but they were sharp, and they'd made headway in areas HEEL had yet to even get near. Rumor said they'd perfected nanotech to act as a booster for latent or weakened magical abilities, though no one had seen any proof yet, not even a prepublished white paper in any of the theoretical journals. When the news hit, HEEL—well, DuMarque, really—had been in a frothing frenzy, as it came right as HEEL announced our own serum entering large-scale trials. While the tech was different—focused on DNA manipulation through low-dose radioisotopes rather than introducing nanites—the outcome was, ostensibly, the same. People who had not evidenced magic, despite being descended from magical lines, were suddenly manifesting abilities.

Allegedly.

No one had seen proof of Halloran and Reynard's work, and HEEL had rushed the last stage of testing to get our serum out there and into limited use.

"What? I bet they would jump at the chance to hire you on and," he brandished his bottle at me like a scepter, "they'd probably be like thirty percent less shitty than HEEL."

I flicked a tiny crumb of cheese at him. "That's not hard to do, all things considered. But Halloran and Reynard Inc. doesn't have the one good thing this new position has going for me."

Royce narrowed his eyes, staring at my face for a long moment before he gasped and sat up straight. "No! Seriously?"

I nodded, my grin impossible to hide. "In the flesh."

"*How*? Oh my God, does he smell as good in person as we thought he would? Are his eyes really that dark? Talk to me!" He punctuated the last three words with slaps to the countertop. "You buried the lede! You should've led with the news you'll be working with Sexy McBowtie, not that you're now part of some weird data entry covert ops team!"

"Drew Hicks, not Office Hottie or Sexy McBowtie. Not if I have to work with him now—I'm afraid I'll fuck up and call him something other than his name." I did my best not to sound like I wanted to sigh his name and doodle hearts in my notebook around our initials. "And the bowtie was one time." Royce had only seen the adorkably hot guy at my work we all had a crush on once, by chance, at a gallery opening Royce dragged me to about a year before. Hicks sauntered in on the arm of a man who could've made Greek statues weep in shame, lingered for about an hour, and then left with his date. Ever since, Royce had been after me for details about him, teasing me frequently about my crush on Drew.

"One *memorable* time." Royce grabbed the bag of tortilla chips and dumped some onto his plate, shoving it and the bowl of guacamole between us. "Now go. Smell, eyes, and is his ass really that round in person, or was that just a trick of gallery lighting?" He held up one hand in a *stop* gesture. "I know you've spoken with him before and been within three feet of him more than once, but this is different. Now you're *in the same department*," he said with dramatic emphasis. "You get to stand right up next to him. So details! Now, please!"

I snorted. "Well, we only got to talk for like five minutes before he had to go to some conference call with DuMarque. *But*," I scraped my chip around the remains of the guac, gathering it up for one big bite, "he's been made co-lad on the project, and that royally pissed off Ivan." That had been a breath of relief. "He's apparently super experienced with the data security end of things and is some sort of data forensics wizard."

"Get to the sexy part!"

"I don't know. I think that's pretty sexy." I don't know what it said about me that I really did. Someone who was not just competent but excellent at something? *Unf.* I had mercy on Royce. "But his eyes really are that dark. Like...if you melted chocolate and mixed it with really good brandy." I'd done my best not to stare at them like some eyeball-obsessed weirdo, but I think he might have noticed because by the time he had to step out and join the conference call, he was doing everything he could not to look me in the face.

"And is he single?" he asked, sounding for all the world like my nosy Aunt Kitty.

"I have no idea," I admitted. "I'm kind of afraid to find out. So long as I don't know for sure, he can exist as a Schrodinger's cat of attainability. Both single and available and probably taken and off limits at the same time."

"Dude..."

"Shut up and let me sublimate my feelings with tortilla chips."

Royce narrowed his eyes, a familiar wicked gleam sparking beneath his lowered lashes. "Just a sec..."

"What are you doing?"

"He's a computer safety boffin, right?"

"Forensic data security." I reached for my beer, frowning when I realized it was empty. How many had I had? I had to go in to work in the morning for a few hours, and a beer headache was only going to make losing a chunk of my weekend worse.

"Same thing. He's the 'you know that password isn't secure' guy. And they go one of two ways," he added, thumb-typing on his phone. "They either think social media is the devil, or they are all over it. And your boy is...ugh, your boy has a stupidly common name."

"Sorry, I'll do better next time. What was that deli guy's name again? Shut Up? Maybe I'll crush on his brother, Go Away."

"Fuck you."

"Oh, wow, that *is* an unusual name. Well, I'll date Fuck You, and you date—"

"Orrin, I love you, but if you keep talking, I will send that stupid dick installation to your office and tell everyone you order your dicks in bulk."

I ate a sad, guacamole-less chip. "Well, I *am* thrifty." I snagged the phone from his grasp and frowned. "Oh my God, why do all these guys think a selfie holding a dead fish is a good idea?"

Our gazes met and locked, similar expressions of dawning horror creeping over both our faces. "No fish, no fish, no fish," we chanted under our breath as we peered at the phone screen, slowly scrolling through the app's *Find Your Friends* feature. "Oh, thank God. No dead fish, no baseball cap, and no mirrored shades."

"Also," Royce pointed out, taking his phone back, "no Drew. At least not *your* Drew."

"Ugh." I peered over his shoulder as he searched on another site, then another. My beer was wearing off, and by the time I started to think maybe stalking my new boss was a weird way to spend my Friday night, Royce made a tiny little sound of victory. "Oh my God, he's a *baby*!"

"The newsletter's only seven years old," he chided. "It's from his alma mater, where he was apparently a member of Kappa Phi Mu for his entire undergrad career, rising in the ranks to become the social director."

We both made a face at that. "He doesn't seem like the guy who'd organize frat parties..."

"Phi Mu is math, right? Or like... academics?" Royce scrolled down the page a bit. "Maybe he organized a mathlympics or something."

"That's not a thing."

"True. You'd totally know if they had mathlympics, my precious little nerd."

"I'd tell you to get fucked, but you're right."

"Ah, here we go. He graduated with honors, his degree in math with a specialization in functional analysis."

"So hot," I sighed, sinking down onto the bar stool next to Royce.

He paused. "You know, it wouldn't be really hard to find his personal phone number."

"That would be stalking," I shot back quickly. Though not before a tiny spark of *do it, do it* flickered to life in my lizard back-brain.

Royce rolled his eyes. "Ugh, you're my Jiminy Cricket."

"You know Pinocchio killed him in the original story? And his name wasn't Jiminy?"

Royce gave me a considering look. "You know, I think I've finally figured out why you never get second dates."

I flicked an errant crumb in his direction. "I don't get second dates because I don't want second dates. It's like going to Costco and actually getting the thirty-pound bag of frozen mini pecan pies instead of just snagging some samples. Sure, the *idea* of all that pie in your freezer is tempting, but you'd get sick of them around pie twelve or thirteen. Then you're stuck with all these pies, and it's not like you can just give your friends an open bag of partially eaten pie—"

He held up one finger. "Did you just compare a romantic partner to food?"

"Mini pecan pies! Which we all know are the best frozen sweet hors d'oeuvres you can buy in bulk."

Royce sighed. "Damn it. Now I want dessert."

He was already over it, but I was feeling unsettled and queasy. "I think you're right."

Royce pushed away from the bar and headed for the freezer, where I knew he kept those super lush spicy chocolate popsicles.

"About dessert?"

"About the project. It's shady as fuck."

I'D HAD MORE THAN THE two beers I'd originally allotted myself at Royce's on Friday night because my head was pounding by the time the first layer of security doors closed behind me on Saturday morning. During the weekend and holidays, the lab facilities ran on a skeleton crew. The Museum to Playing God on the ground floor was open to the public but usually fairly empty, save for a handful of employees working on exhibits and the errant family or two wandering through, hoping to get the kids interested in something educational rather than whatever kids were into that parents disapproved of. After my scan, the second layer of doors hissed open, deeming me safe to enter the building through the employee doors. The pop of the airlock releasing made the back of my eyeballs throb.

Thankfully, the bright lights of the corridor were dimmed due to the weekend hours, but the lobby I had to cross was made entirely of glass panels and let in the subtropical autumn sun without mercy. I'd asked my coworker Mina how much it cost to cool the place, and she'd just laughed, telling me that if I knew, I'd probably cry. I wished for the sunglasses I'd forgotten on the little antique piecrust table by my front door. With a deep breath to fortify myself, I rushed from the narrow corridor and across the expansive lobby, heading for the bank of employees-only elevators tucked away near the maintenance access doors behind a rather rabid attack ficus, similar to the one I had in my office.

I may or may not have liberated said office attack ficus from the lobby a few months ago in a fit of pique regarding my placement in the former storage closet.

The museum part of the ground floor seemed mostly empty as I scurried across the lobby. Other than the security guard by the building's inner door and Linda at the front desk, the only people other than myself were a small clump of teenagers surrounding one harried-looking adult, who was lecturing about the Star Fall sparking magic to life centuries ago, and one small figure wearing a coat entirely too heavy for the weather. This person lingered by the awkward hologram HEEL had centered at the museum's entrance, depicting a man in a lab coat staring proudly at some spot out the front door. A shooting star, supposed to symbolize the union of science and magic, danced over his head, zipping back and forth at irregular intervals.

Allegedly.

I thought the man bore a strong resemblance to DuMarque and had some *thoughts* about that.

"Excuse me. Are you Orrin Grimm?"

So close... I glanced longingly at the dull gray elevator doors, painted to blend in with the walls. Fingering my keycard, I wondered if I could put on some Olympic-level burst of speed and make it into the elevator before having to talk with the person bearing down on me.

“You are, right? Orrin Grimm?”

I forced myself to try to at least look neutral, if not pleasant, and turned to see the small figure in the heavy coat hurrying toward me. “I am. Can I help you?”

They smiled thinly, showing the very edge of a neat row of square teeth set into a very wizened, sun-darkened face. “I’m supposed to speak with you today.”

I glanced up at Linda, busy doing whatever it was she did when she was pretending not to notice things going on around her. The guard by the door was operating one of the outer security portals, leaving only the harried-looking adult with their murder of teenagers to tell me what the hell was going on.

They were no help, seeing as how they were now busy examining the hands-on display where they could handle bits of (very inert, no danger to the public) meteor from the site of the Star Fall.

“I’m sorry. I thought we were scheduled to talk later.” I hoped the smile I was forcing was professional and not a grimace of pain. “You're a bit early, but once Mr. Hicks gets here, we can get started.”

“I’m supposed to speak with you,” they repeated, their smile fixed. “Now, because I need to go soon.”

“Er, okay. Let’s head up to the conference room, then.” Drew had texted me (and I had totally not squeed about it. Totally.) to let me know he’d reserved the cozier of the conference rooms for our first round of interviews. Not only was it less intimidating because of its small size, it was literally right next door to the on-site lab we used for employee physicals and would facilitate gathering the samples from our interviewees. If they only had to go three feet, way less chance of them promising to go to their doctor’s office or the one chain of labs in the area and bailing or forgetting.

“No.” Their hand closed around my elbow, a shock of heat spreading from where their palm met my bare skin. “Now.”

Fuck my life. I couldn't remember their name; Drew had also sent me a list of the first-round interviewees, all culled from DuMarque's list, but I couldn't recall a single one of them. In fact, I could barely remember anything. My head buzzed with a high-pitched electric whine, reminding me of that gross purple bug light Mom's friend Karla kept on her back porch to murder moths. It wasn't pain but something like it creeping up my neck, crawling over my chest as I stared down at the person in front of me, their expression unchanging. Their voice was unfamiliar to me, but I still knew I was hearing them in my head when the words came.

Jim says hello. Jim says run fast.

They let go of my arm, and sound came rushing back with a physical *whump* sensation, making me gasp and setting me back a few steps. The sudden lack of buzzing in my head, of heat in my arm, was disorienting. "What the Hell!"

Linda lifted her head from whatever she'd been looking at and frowned. "You okay, Orrin?"

The figure in the heavy coat was gone. Not disappeared because that would be too weird. They were already past the guard, though, and hustling through the series of security doors to the street. "Hey!" I took a step toward the guard, stopping when everything tried to shift sideways without my permission.

"Sit down." Linda came out from behind reception and grabbed one of the rolly chairs to bring over to me. "Drew! Thank God—something's wrong with Orrin!"

Drew's face moved into view. With a soft thump, he dropped his messenger bag and jacket, and then he was bending over me, checking my pulse in my neck and scowling. "Can you grab him something sweet to drink? I think there's juice in the employee locker room fridge down here."

Linda nodded and was gone before I could stop her.

"I'm not going to faint." I tried to shake him off and failed. Digging my heels in, I managed to push the rolly chair back a few inches, but instead of shaking Drew's grasp, he moved with me.

And damned if a tiny part of me didn't like that.

"Tell me what happened." Scanning my face for something, he gripped my chin lightly between his thumb and forefinger. Linda was back, holding an icy cold can of pineapple juice. "Thanks," he murmured. "You're wonderful."

Laughing, she flapped her hand at him. "Oh, don't try to butter me up, Drew Hicks. I'm still not validating your parking." She gave me one more bemused, less concerned glance before returning to her desk.

The group in the museum was hidden between the displays now, but their voices bounced around us in fragments, snippets of conversation and at least one teenager sighing and complaining about how boring it all was. Drew dropped his hand but didn't move back. "Take a drink." He pressed the cold can into my hand. "You looked ready to faint a minute ago. Tell me what happened, and then if you need to go to the hospital—"

"I don't. Seriously. I feel fine now." And I did. Except that stupid fluttering in my gut whenever I saw Drew had intensified with proximity. "Just some weird guy." I trailed off. How did I even explain it? *Some stranger came up to me, and I felt like a bug zapper, heard their voice in my head, and really, I'm fine?* Yeah, that'd go over real well. "I guess maybe it was my blood sugar or something."

"Weird guy? Where?" He craned his head, glancing toward the museum and then the exit doors. "Where did he go?"

I shook my head. "He took off out the front doors right before I went down. He's long gone. And he didn't hurt me," I added, though I wasn't sure if that was the whole truth. "It was just a...a thing. He's gone, I'm fine. I swear." I shifted uneasily. "I'm fine," I repeated. It had to be true—whatever had just happened had to be because of my lack of sleep or that third beer the night before. *Maybe something was wrong with the guacamole.*

He gave me a long, considering stare. "Keep sipping that. Let's get up to the conference room and get started."

"ACCORDING TO THE INITIAL report, Sarah was witnessed changing a folded piece of paper into an actual flower for a customer's son. Another witness reports she spoiled a package of raw chicken by passing her hand over it when a customer was verbally abusive to one of the cashiers around closing time," he murmured as we headed for the conference room where our first interview was waiting. "But there's been no solid evidence of anything. It's hearsay."

I nodded, pausing when we got to the door. "We're doing this the usual way, I take it?"

"Why mess with a good thing?" Pushing the door open, he gestured for me to go ahead.

The young woman who could only get time to come in on a Saturday was harried, with dark circles under her eyes so deep I thought they were bruises at first. Eyes darting between Drew and me rabbit quick, she kept smoothing her hands over the long, thick plait slung forward over her shoulder. "Are you sure you're up for this?" I asked gently. "I know Doctor DuMarque said it was important, but if you're not willing—"

"No, no, I'm fine." She smiled, plastic and tight. If I sounded that unbelievable with Drew, no wonder he was giving me the fisheye. "I just had a late shift last night. I work at Epicurious doing overnights." She shrugged. "It's not what I wanted to do, but they have a voucher program for childcare."

Drew finally looked away, making a note on his tablet. "Do you understand why you were asked to come in, Miss Green?"

"Sarah." Her smile was more genuine this time. "And it's because my mom was magical, right? She was a telepath."

"Was?"

Sarah winced. I reached for the cheap box of tissues on the conference room desk and set it unobtrusively next to her arm, resting on the table. A series of old, thin scars ran jaggedly from her elbow to the top of her hand, like a big cat had gotten hold of her years ago. She saw me notice them and drew her arm away, tucking it under the table on her lap. "She died when I was about seven. It was fast. She was fine one day and then," she snapped her fingers, "gone."

"My dad died when I was four," I said quietly. "Fast for him, too. He got sick with something, and before we knew it, he'd passed away."

She nodded. "That's how it was with Mom." She shifted uncomfortably. "I used to think... I used to think someone killed her, you know? Because who wants to believe their mom can just die like that? It had to be some nefarious plot, right?" She laughed weakly. "Because when you're seven, that sort of shit doesn't happen." A small shrug. "At least that's what I thought then. Now I know better. Sometimes life is shit."

"Sarah," I said before Drew could resume his questioning, "you're here because there's been some question as to whether or not you inherited your mother's abilities."

Sarah went still for a second. It wasn't even a full heartbeat of a moment, but it was enough to notice. "I definitely didn't," she said with a watery laugh. "If I had, do you think I'd be busting my ass in a rich people grocery store, stocking shitty overpriced marinara and fucking," she waved one hand angrily, "squid ink pasta and shit?"

"What would you be doing?" Drew leaned back in his chair, shifting that intense stare to Sarah now.

"Same thing she did," Sarah shot back. "I'd work for one of the companies competing to hire magicals. There's so few of them left, they get paid fucking bank. If I had even a sliver of her ability, of *any* ability, my kid wouldn't be wearing worn-out shoes I got from Goodwill and diapers someone donated to the church." She sniffed in irritation, bringing both hands up to scrub at her face. "Look, it's fucking obvious I'm not running around bippity-boppity-booing shit, okay? Look at my *life*, for fuck's sake! How many magicals are out there on assistance, damn near on the verge of tricking to make sure their kid has food for the next week?"

"Grocery stores don't pay well?" Drew asked quietly.

We both stared at him for a long, fraught moment. "Not usually," I said before Sarah could reply. "Especially if you're a single parent."

Sarah made a miserable sound, something between a laugh and a growl. "It's not only that. I can't get insurance through work, you know? They keep us barely under full-time hours, so they don't have to let us have it. And the state shit?" She snorted. Even Drew nodded in commiseration; we all knew how godawful the options were in Texas. "If I had even the tiniest bit of magic," she sighed, the fight fading and exhaustion creeping over her features, "you can fucking bet your ass I wouldn't be here right now. Me and my baby would be far away. Safe." She fidgeted. "I heard there's some of those intentional living communities starting up for people in my situation. Where it's, you know, safe for us."

"Safe," I repeated.

Drew was frowning at his tablet, no doubt wondering how to get us back on track with the questions we were supposed to be asking.

I scooted closer to Sarah to block her view of him. "Are you not safe now, Sarah? Do you need help?"

"Not from the lab," she said softly.

Huh?

She darted a glance at Drew over my shoulder before turning her attention back to me. "I'm not gifted," she said with a sort of finality, speaking years of fading hope and, finally, acceptance. "But my kid might be, okay? She was tested when she was born, but the results were inconclusive."

Behind me, Drew had gone very still. Inconclusive results didn't happen often. The chances were vanishingly rare, in fact. "Did they retest her?"

Sarah lifted the corner of one lip in a snarl. "Do I look like I could pay for a retest? We're on public aid. We get one test, one doctor visit, one dentist visit per year. Anything outside of the bare minimum is out of pocket."

"You're in luck then," Drew interrupted. "As part of this interview, we're requesting a blood sample and a urine sample. We can retest you and, if the results suggest it's necessary, arrange for your daughter to be retested as well at no cost."

"Why don't we get that part over with?" I stood and held out a hand for Sarah to take. "Then we can do the rest of these boring questions. Drew, could you go grab us a drink from the break room? I don't know about you," I pitched my voice lower, as if imparting a great confidence to Sarah, while I led her gently but firmly toward the conference room door, "but I always get so woozy with blood draws. Having something sweet right after really helps."

Sarah wilted into herself, her left hand moving to cover the scars on her right arm in an absentminded way, old habit rather than fresh discomfort. "How much blood are they going to need? Is it going to take long?"

The answer was *a lot, all things considered* and *longer than you'd like,* but I merely smiled and gave her arm a squeeze. "What's your little girl's name?"

"Charlotte." She told me all about how much Charlotte loved to draw, and, even though she was barely two, she was pretty sure the kiddo had real talent. That led to a long story about the preschool she was able to get Charlotte into with the voucher from her job and how much better it was than the shitty storefront place near their apartment, where the teachers were never the same two weeks in a row and it always smelled like industrial cleaner and wet graham crackers. "This place she's at smells like lavender and fucking oatmeal." She beamed as Benny, the tech on duty for the half-day interview session, glanced up at her with a wide-eyed sort of admiration.

Sarah barely glanced his way as Benny switched out vials to collect samples and racked them in his cart before, blushing, handing her the small plastic urine sample cup and directing her to the small bathroom in the lab itself. As soon as the door shut behind me, Benny whipped around to face me, a question already forming on his lips.

Fuck.

AFTER THE TRIP TO THE lab, Sarah managed to get through the actual interview just fine, like something in her settled once the lab work part was done. I had to wonder if that had something to do with how Benny shyly complimented her, told her she was doing better than the people he worked with daily would when it was time for their tests, and generally praised her from sunrise to sunset as he casually labeled her cup of pee and gushed about her band t-shirt. I refused to try and "do my thing," as Benny had asked before Sarah emerged from the bathroom, and I was saved from any begging by Drew, who'd popped in to see what was taking so long.

His fisheye had intensified, though, as we finally got through all the questions with Sarah. We had a small gap in the middle of her interview and the next—a guy named Niall, reportedly reading minds in his college dorm—and the silence between us was uncomfortable. I fiddled with my own tablet, making notes about Sarah's interview and my observations on her behavior and demeanor.

"Hey," I said into the quiet, "did something seem off about her to you? Not her-her, but just...like some of the things she said? Like not wanting the help the lab could give because she didn't want to be part of it and going somewhere else..."

Setting his tablet aside, Drew fixed me with a considering gaze that did *things* to me. Things that should not happen in an office conference room because anywhere slideshows came to die was not the place to pop a boner. "She was nervous, and nervous people ramble. And nervous people sometimes like to put up a wall of bravado. She didn't want us feeling bad for her even while she felt bad for herself. She loves her kid and didn't want us to think she felt any other way, so she threw up that front made of piss and vinegar."

A funny feeling—one I'd had before but never in this situation—rushed through me. Hot and cold at once, with the sensation of everything in the room tilting sideways even while I stood still. And, oddly, the taste of cold watermelon emerged in the back of my throat, the same feeling I got whenever I knew people were meant for one another. The same cold certainty that, if they decided to pursue something, it would work. I couldn't say if it would be easy or hard, but it would end up working out well.

But why was I feeling that now, I wondered, when I wasn't in a situation calling for the use of my weird little ability?

The only reason I could come up with was that we were talking about Sarah, and my brain was still circling around that surge of certainty when Benny asked if I thought he should ask her out. Swallowing down that watermelon taste, I shook myself and refocused on Drew, who was giving me a very intense frown. "What?"

"You went all weird for a second. I think maybe—"

"I'm fine!"

He shook his head. "I don't like that you had that funny spell, earlier. While you were with Sarah in the lab, I called down to security to see if they could pull tapes and—"

"You *what*? Oh my God..." I was torn between flattered he cared that much and embarrassment I was now officially part of a *thing*, a *thing* that would probably get me called on the carpet in front of DuMarque and involve paperwork and questions and a lot of side-eyeing and oh my god...

Drew leaned back in his chair. "Why don't you want this looked into?"

"Because it's embarrassing," I admitted. Though that was only part of it. I was also afraid. "I just had a weird spell, is all."

"Someone confronted you—"

"It was hardly a confrontation!"

"Legally—"

"You're a lawyer now?"

He narrowed his eyes at me. "Orrin, what else happened downstairs? It was something different than what you told me, wasn't it?"

"Oh, you're a psychic lawyer to boot!" The flash of annoyance in his eyes was at once viscerally satisfying and shameful. "Fucking hell. Look, I'm fine, okay? I don't want security getting involved."

"Well, you don't have to worry," he said coolly. "They couldn't see anything on the tapes. Whatever happened was in a blind spot."

"What?"

He made a thoughtful humming noise. "Convenient for your would-be assailant, hm? They didn't see what happened, just a small figure in a heavy coat heading for the doors." Frowning, he rifled through his paper files. "Niall is running late."

Quiet settled between us, uncomfortable and thick as cotton wool. After several minutes marked by the loudly ticking clock over the conference room door, I couldn't take it anymore. "You don't really think that about Sarah, do you? That she was fronting?" I was certain she wasn't, that something underlying was bothering her. Something she wanted to talk about but couldn't.

Drew hesitated, then sighed long and soft, an almost sleepy sound tugging at something funny inside me. He sounded tired. Tired and frustrated. "It doesn't matter what I think. What we're here for is data, not feelings."

Yikes.

"But your feelings can definitely affect the data collection. If our subject feels threatened, they get defensive. If they feel supported..." I spread my hands. "We get better results."

Drew fixed me with a gimlet eye. "That's why we work so well together." He surprised me into a blush. "You're good at making the subjects feel supported. And that's what DuMarque is hoping for with this new department, when we take our show on the road."

I made a face. "It feels hella invasive, you know? Going to track people down and ask them our list of personal questions and collect bodily fluids. Wait—"

"Ah, that's part two of our day." He anticipated my question with a slight, awkward frown. "We have a brief training session with Benny on administering blood sample tests, collecting urine specimens, and storing them."

"Is the lab providing us with a company car or anything?"

"Er, no?"

"And we have to transport bodily fluid samples?" He nodded. "One, two, three, not it! We're taking your car for this shit."

A soft knock interrupted whatever he'd been about to say, but as our next subject stepped in, Drew grinned down at his tablet.

THE INTERVIEWS HAD been boilerplate boring, except Sarah's still niggled at me as Benny walked us through basic blood collection procedure and made us practice on one another. Hesitant but gentle, Drew took a blood sample from me and placed it in the rack. I was less lucky, blowing a vein in one of his arms before Benny showed me how to use a butterfly needle, which was smaller and easier for me to handle.

"This feels like something a qualified professional should be doing. Isn't there a lab we can farm this out to?" My face and throat were clammy, and my stomach roiled at the sight of Drew's blood trickling into the prepared vial.

"Well," Benny drawled, hissing under his breath when I forgot how to take the needle out properly and squirted blood on Drew's shirt. "Technically, yes, but DuMarque is all about streamlining lately, and loopholes allow for the two of you to collect the samples after approved training, with the proviso you don't misrepresent yourselves as healthcare professionals." He glanced up at me, his own cheeks coloring slightly. "So, um, the samples from today should be through analysis by Tuesday at the latest..."

"If it's all good," I pressed a cotton pad to Drew's abused arm, "she'll be released from the interview cohort after the results are recorded."

Benny nodded, already smiling and no doubt planning how to ask Sarah out. He hadn't asked me for her contact information, though. Not that I'd have given it; even if it hadn't been a violation of about a dozen laws and regulations, it was a personal matchmaking policy of mine. If you wanted to talk to someone, do it yourself. Figure it out on your own.

Drew and I cleaned ourselves up and dropped our tablets off in IT before taking the elevator down to the main floor. The museum area was empty save for one of the cleaning staff running a polisher over the floor and Linda at the front desk, packing up and getting ready to head home herself. "Did you drive?" Drew asked suddenly.

"Um. Ever or specifically today?"

Because my default setting is smartass, apparently.

His lips tilted a tiny bit up to one side. "Today."

"I took the light rail and walked from the McAllen stop." I shrugged. "It was early enough to miss the suburbanite influx."

"But it's probably not now." Drew didn't quite meet my eyes. "Um, I drove. Would you...would you like a ride home?"

I opened my mouth to say *no thanks, I don't mind walking a bit, but I appreciate the offer*. Some god watching over me intervened, though, and instead, I said, "Sure, I'd love that. Thanks."

That time, he definitely, undoubtedly, smiled.

Chapter Five

DREW

Orrin lived in the Warehouse District. While it was the focus of some pretty intense development and a push for new money to move in and snap up the overpriced lofts with charming views of either a baseball stadium or more warehouses, it also had clusters of actual old warehouses, converted to apartments before the efforts to revitalize downtown really took root.

"Sorry," he muttered as my poor Forester jolted and rattled over what had once been a utility alley between the old cracker factory and an auto body shop built sometime in the fifties, now a row of shops with an industrial aesthetic. "I'm pretty sure the city is hoping we'll all move out once we get tired of replacing car parts. Then they can let the developers swoop in on our little corner."

As he spoke, he gestured at the former factory turned apartments. The place was a long, low building, only three stories compared to the towering residences looking over the block from either side. Originally painted some orange and red design, it had faded to a buttery, sandy yellow with traces of the original cracker company logo peeking through swaths of complicated, surprisingly beautiful graffiti. "Wow."

He glanced at me, his expression carefully neutral. "I like it. It's definitely not somewhere I ever imagined living when I was younger, but now I can't think of anywhere else I'd rather be." He motioned toward a curbside parking spot. "It's not metered on weekends. If you want to pull in there, I can hop out, and you can go enjoy the rest of your weekend."

I executed an only slightly shameful parallel parking job. I was loathe to let him out of the car, but I couldn't think of any good reason to ask him to linger. Suggesting lunch felt too forward, too much like a date. It was too early for drinks (at least for me), and asking if I could come up and see his place...definitely felt like after-date territory. "So..."

"So where are we supposed to go for our first out of town trip?" he asked in a rush, fiddling with the edge of his seatbelt. "DuMarque was supposed to send us an email yesterday, but I never got it, so..."

"Oh! Um. Just to Beaumont, so not too far. We're blocked out for the entire day, though."

He nodded. "Traffic."

"Traffic. Yep."

Beaumont required driving on some of the worst freeways I'd ever been on in terms of traffic and the laissez-faire attitude of the drivers. We could conceivably dart out and back by lunchtime, but...well. I didn't want to think too hard on why I pushed for the outing to get scheduled for a full day block when DuMarque had suggested only a four-hour trip.

Orrin unbuckled and bent to gather up his ever-present messenger bag and laptop. "So, I guess see you Monday? I mean, if things change, you can text me."

"I don't have your personal number. Only your work one."

He popped up, eyes wide as some expression I couldn't name darted across his features. "Here, hand me your phone and let me text myself. Then you'll have it."

When I fished my phone out of my pocket, he plucked it from my fingers, tapping a quick *Hi. It's me*, and hitting send. I grinned at the screen. "I figure we'll head out after rush hour. We might not get back till late, though."

"Traffic," he repeated. Licking his lips, he eyed me with consideration. "Um, if you want to, maybe we can leave earlier? Pick me up here, and we can hit I-10 easier. It's right up the road. There's an old on-ramp..." He trailed off. "I mean, it's a thought."

More time with Orrin, outside of work? "$ure. We can sort out details this weekend."

"Right, right." He popped open the door and stuck one leg out. "I'm sure I'm keeping you from plans. Dates. Outings. Tuxedos or something. So. Text me and I'll text you and I'm just gonna get going now bye."

The final words all came out in one breath, ending on a small gasp as he slid the rest of his body from the car, shutting the door before I could even formulate a reply. He walked—one of those restrained gaits saying someone was trying not to run—all the way to the double metal doors of the building, tapped in a code quickly, and, with a backward glance and a startle when he saw me watching, squeezed himself between the barely open door and the frame. In a dull thud of metal, he disappeared from sight.

I thumbed my phone open and pulled up his message. Adding his name to the number, I hesitated a moment before tapping out, *Thanks for coming in today. We're good together.*

Only after I hit send did I realize the phrasing could be sorely misconstrued.

And maybe... maybe I wouldn't mind if it was.

THE REST OF SATURDAY passed in a weird state of excited nervousness, interspersed with long periods of feeling like an absolute tool for being excited about a business trip only because I found the coworker going with me to be attractive.

But he seemed to be, I don't know, flirting a little, didn't he?

Don't be weird, Drew. Just because a guy is shy, or nice, or both doesn't mean he's into you and harboring a secret crush.

But...maybe?

"Ugh!" I threw myself down on the slick, black leather sofa my interior decorator had chosen to match with the sleek silver-and-white palette of my apartment. Then I had a moment of feeling like an absolute douchebag thinking about having paid an interior designer an obscene amount of money to make my home look like Hell's waiting room. Cool, sleek lines and cold lack of color had made me feel very adult and professional for all of ten minutes, until the first time I tried to relax on the damned sofa and nearly slid off onto the cold, rugless floor.

Because a nice, soft rug would have ruined the aesthetic, apparently.

I thought of Orrin's funky apartment building. Was his apartment as colorful and unique as the outside had suggested? Seeing him at work, wearing the typical office uniform of a button-up, tie, and slacks, didn't suggest anything bohemian or unusual about his decorating tastes, but I had a pretty strong feeling he had at least a few fandom posters on his walls and more than one bookcase full of an eclectic mix of reading material and not the chrome-and-glass floating shelves lining one wall of my Midtown penthouse. The books were all covered in slick black paper, their jackets removed and replaced by essentially expensive paper bags to give the shelves a "uniform, neutral appearance."

I honestly had no idea what books were under the covers or if they were even really books. My *real* reading material was divided between my e-reader, several special storage boxes beneath my bed, and a climate-controlled unit in the complex's lower level. There, I kept my precious first editions and some old, tattered childhood favorites so well-read, they were virtually falling apart.

For a while, the colorless and cool lines of my apartment had been annoying but comforting at the same time. I didn't "people" well, and I felt best when everything was very tidy and organized. What didn't work for me was the lack of depth, of feeling in the place. From time to time, I wondered if the designer had been mocking me after I told her that I preferred clean lines and didn't like fuss.

And why was I obsessing about it all? I pulled a leather throw pillow over my face to block out the glare of the late afternoon sun pouring through the floor-to-ceiling windows.

Because you're comparing yourself to Orrin and wondering if he could even stand someone as boring as you.

Shut up, brain. You're not helping.

Chapter Six

ORRIN

The weird, unsettled feeling that had come over me after Sarah's interview flickered on and off all weekend, leaving me feeling queasy and exhausted by the time Drew pulled up early Monday morning, before the sun peeked through the tall buildings around my apartment. Royce tried to insist on waiting with me, "just in case he turns out to be a serial killer or something." When I reminded him he was allergic to sunrise and if Drew *were* going to turn me into a skin coat, he wasn't going to do it in front of my apartment but wait until he got me out of town at least, Royce relented. Nevertheless, he made me promise to text him multiple times and use the code word *chartreuse* if things got weird.

I loved my best friend, but sometimes I thought about getting him a puppy, something he could lavish attention on and let me breathe.

Watching Drew try to finagle his Forester into a spot down the sidewalk from the front of my building, I felt my phone vibrate and nearly ignored it. On the second vibration, I sighed and pulled it out of my pocket to see *Unknown Number* instead of Royce's glitter-streaked face, his profile pic I took when we went to Mardi Gras in college.

Drew had wedged his vehicle into the parking spot and was out, opening the rear door and shoving his overnight bag to one side, fiddling around the way people do when they're not sure how to act before a road trip. I glanced at my still-vibrating phone and sighed, setting it to silent mode before shoving it back into my front pocket. If it wasn't Royce, it could wait. Anything work-related, they'd call my work phone, which was safely in my satchel with the ringer set to an unmissable, shrill pattern.

"You okay there?" I called as Drew moved his bag back to the other side again. "Or is this some sort of pre-drive ritual you need privacy for?"

He lifted his head and, with two high spots of color on his cheeks, shrugged. "Just making sure you have enough room." He eyed my small overnight bag, one of his dark brows creeping upward.

"I'm going to pretend your surprise at my failure to overpack isn't kind of insulting," I said mildly, dropping my bag into the wide-open cargo area.

Those spots of color grew deeper. "Sorry, I just thought you might..."

"Be fussy? Insist on wardrobe changes throughout the day?" I was being kind of a dick, and I knew it, but I couldn't stop myself from pressing. "Do you really think I'm like that?"

Drew's mouth worked mutely, but then he stopped, raised a brow, and fixed me with a cool, sharp look. "Are you saying there's something wrong with people who are?"

"Touché," I laughed, startled. "No, there's not. I'm just more of a dick than usual today. I'm sorry." He was right; there wasn't anything wrong with overpacking, and how much it bothered me he thought *I* could be like that was unsettling. I thought of Royce and his tendency to pack an entire luggage set for an overnight trip to Galveston and how my mother would make sure her purse was absolutely bulging with "just in case" items whenever she left the house, ensuring she was safe in any eventuality, from smeared lipstick to nuclear winter.

"I was just surprised you had that image of me in your head, I suppose." I stood back so he could shut the door. "Though why you'd have any image of me in your head is kind of a mystery, too."

Drew glanced sidelong at me but said nothing. After a moment, he moved to the driver's side and popped the locks. We got underway. Drew followed my murmured directions to the old on-ramp to I-10, a trash-strewn ramp curving at a breathtaking angle, hidden under a muddle of fencing and old signs, overgrown with surprisingly beautiful morning glory vines. As we waited for the metered light to change to green so we could get on the freeway, Drew noticed me looking at the just-opening flowers. "Those are pretty."

"It's actually one of my favorite things about living here. The area looks scuzzy on the outside edges, but there are these hidden beautiful things. Like the morning glories. They're everywhere, and most people think they're just trash vines." I sighed. "They're considered an invasive plant, and the city or county goes around lopping them down, but they're resilient, really, and always come back."

The light changed, and Drew sped up the ramp, leaving the purple and blue blooms behind. Even though it was barely sunrise, the freeway was packed. I lived in the middle of downtown—the old part, not the shiny, glossy part they liked to put on brochures and use as a backdrop on news stories—and I-10 was one of the busiest roads in the state, especially where it cut through Houston. Drew handled traffic deftly, merging and braking with a sort of calm grace I envied.

"You're staring," he murmured after fifteen or so minutes during which we'd barely made it to the next on-ramp.

"I'm wondering how you're doing this without cursing everyone's mother. When I do drive, I'm a mess in minutes. Especially on the freeway."

Drew smiled faintly. "That surprises me about you. You always seem so cool and collected at work."

I snorted. "Your interactions with me at work have been very limited."

"Well, I've seen enough to know you're not going to fly off the handle at one of our subjects if they get shirty with us. Every time we've bumped into each other, you've been very...chill."

"Even on Saturday? You seemed pretty annoyed with me then."

Drew grunted, going quiet as he wove us in and out of a traffic jam and into the surprisingly clear stretch of freeway ahead of a fender bender. "I wasn't annoyed at you," he said finally. "I was...frustrated at a situation."

"Hm. Well, to be honest, so was I. I think we should look more into what Sarah said about going somewhere. Something about it..." I shook my head. "I just have a feeling."

"A feeling?" He clicked his tongue dismissively. "Feelings aren't facts, Orrin, and we have to focus on just facts right now. *Feelings* lead to people getting reported as unregistered magicals. Some of Sarah's coworkers had a feeling she was hiding something or maybe a feeling she didn't belong at that job. I can bet actual folding money that, no matter what our findings are, Sarah's boss is going to have a *feeling* she's too much trouble to keep on and let her go."

He was right. I didn't like it, but he was right.

"If I were king of the world," I said quietly, watching the University of Houston slip past my window, "I would make it illegal for people to require testing for a job. Or housing. I would make it illegal to prioritize magic over the person."

Drew made a noise between a groan and a sigh. "That would be ideal but unrealistic. The world's been like this too long to suddenly unmake it."

"Well, as the chances of me being king of the world are slim, you have nothing to worry about," I said tartly. "Trust me, I know this is how the world works. My parents..." The words dried out in my throat. I didn't talk much about my mother with anyone other than Royce and definitely never my father. But when I looked at Drew, that fizzy fuzzy watermelon feeling bubbled in my veins. Calm washed over me, not sedating me so much as grounding me, making me feel safe even as he swerved around an eighteen-wheeler determined to take out a swathe of Houston's compact cars.

Trust him, my thoughts whispered. *It's not like it's a secret, is it? Even if you wished it were.*

"My parents used to work for the lab, back when it first got started. Back when DuMarque and, er, Halloran and Reynard started it, in fact. They worked out of the old facility, the one the university let them lease." He didn't look at me, keeping his eyes fixed on the road stretching out toward Beaumont. "Anyway, my dad, he, um...he was telekinetic. He got really sick and died when I was little, but before that, he'd worked with DuMarque, and when Halloran and Reynard left, Dad was sort of the unofficial official co-lead researcher."

Drew visibly stiffened. "Oh?"

"You already knew about my parents, didn't you?" When he hesitated, I huffed an annoyed breath. "Don't lie. You already knew."

"A little," he admitted. "Just from the lobby museum. I didn't, you know, Google you or something." He finally darted a glance my way. "Promise."

That fizzy fuzzy watermelon feeling tickled again. He was being truthful.

I nodded. "Thank you for being honest with me. A few people liked to pretend it was all news to them while at the same time pumping me for information, trying to get some inside gossip or something, things never part of the official story." When I was a kid, it was worse. My father's death lingered in the news cycles for a while—a golden child of the Revive project, dead by mysterious circumstances at such a young age, his wife quitting the lab where they'd worked together... The public loved conspiracy theories, and my family ended up being the center of a few.

His grin was back. "True. Well, in the spirit of honesty—"

"I haven't had enough coffee for honesty," I grumbled. "Can we maybe go with half-truths and white lies?"

"Hush. In the spirit of honesty, I guess I should admit I'm terrible at the whole interpersonal thing, and you're saving my ass, coming on this trip and...well, and not quitting when DuMarque moved you to the department."

I shook my head a little. "I have to admit, I get a real weird feeling about this whole thing."

Drew shrugged again. "It's just growing pains. HEEL is the only lab in the world with the reach to expand a Revive project like this, and the potential threat of industrial espionage—"

I couldn't stop the snort escaping.

"You don't think that's a potential threat?" His brows creeped up. "And I'm stopping for coffee. You want any?"

"Yes, all of it," I groaned. "And I think the idea someone out there has developed a similar technology to strengthen latent magical abilities or is somehow creating new ones in previously mundane people is ridiculous. Let's be real here—we both know DuMarque is chomping at the bit to accuse Halloran and Reynard of wrongdoing. It's driving him nuts that he can't pin it on them already."

"You really think that?" He took the next exit, slowing as we merged into feeder road traffic. "I'm...I'm kind of shocked."

"I'm not." Even as I said the words aloud, I realized this was the first time I'd voiced it to anyone other than Royce, who didn't even work in a lab-adjacent field and would have no horse in the race. Still, I couldn't stop myself from rambling on. "Halloran and Reynard have been lowkey for decades. Their lab is barely a blip on any scientific radar. All their funding comes from private donations. They don't have the resources to even play on the same field as HEEL, much less engage in some complex industrial espionage and administer the Revive serum willy-nilly."

Drew turned into the fast food joint's parking lot, swinging into the first available spot and parking. He shut off the engine before replying. "I don't think you're wrong, but I think there's more to these possible magicals running around unregistered and untested than DuMarque is admitting. And as things stand? The lab isn't the only group keeping track of positive tests. At least three government entities in each country involved in the Star Fall Treaty track reports of surprise magic use."

It was my turn to grunt. "We're getting off the point. Coffee first, then..." I trailed off.

"Then we need to discuss these interviews. What do you want? I'll go in. It'll be faster than waiting in the drive-through line."

I gave him my order—black, obscene amounts of sugar, and enough milk to make it beige—and dug out my phone while he went into the restaurant. There were six texts from Royce and three from *Unknown Number*. Royce's were all the same: ***Call me, Asshole.***

Seeing Drew was still in line inside, I called Royce and got his voicemail. "You wanted me to call you 'asshole' so here I am, calling you asshole. I'll let you know when we get to the hotel later. Love you bunches." Still smiling and thinking about Royce's reaction to the message, I hung up and opened one of the unknown number texts.

Jim says hello.

Jim says you're not hidden now.

Jim says get ready to run.

My stomach sank so far, I thought it was somewhere around my left boot heel. Hands shaking, I fired off a text to Royce. ***Did you send me messages trying to be funny?***

A minute later, he replied. ***Got your voicemail, asshole. And I don't try to be funny; I am funny.***

Seriously. I got some weird messages from an unknown number. Was that you?

My phone rang. "And just when would I have had the time to do something like that? I'm at work. Arranging dicks."

"I'm halfway to Beaumont," I said. "Checkmate."

"You're right. That *is* worse. Now tell me about these messages. Could it be one of your exes acting like a jerk?"

With a sigh, I gave him a rundown of the texts. "But okay, here's the weirder part. On Saturday, I had a, um...I guess you could call it a run-in with someone at work." I told him about the strange, small figure who cornered me and the voice I heard saying basically the same thing as the texts.

Royce was quiet for a long moment. Long enough for Drew to pay for our drinks and step aside to wait for the cups. Finally, Royce sighed. "Either someone is going to great lengths to fuck with you, or maybe...maybe it's time you talked to your mom again."

"OKAY, GO OVER THE LIST again," Drew ordered. We were nearly at the hotel, and he'd already called ahead to make sure the conference room was set up for our interviews. Now he wanted to review everything we knew about the subjects before we got there. Traffic meant we were cutting it perilously close time-wise and wouldn't have time to relax in our rooms for a few minutes beforehand and review notes.

"Three interviews," I repeated. "First up is Cameron Diggs. Age twenty-six. Alleged evidence of pyrokinesis."

"Yikes."

I smirked. "You said that the past three times. But the evidence is extremely thin. His parents have no positive testing history. The last known magical in the Diggs family was Obadiah Diggs in 1901, and he was telekinetic. On Cameron's mother's side, there has never been a history of magic."

"Next."

"Rebecca Morse. Alleged Changeling."

"I'm sorry, a what now?"

"Changeling. Rarest of the rare, magically. There's only five known Changelings in the entire world, and only one in the U.S." Changelings weren't actual faerie children living amongst humans, but the phrase had been used for centuries. The name had gotten attached to magic users who were able to convince others they weren't seeing what was directly in front of them, altering perceptions, even altering their own appearance through the power of suggestion. The moniker stuck, even after the renaming movements over the past ninety years. "She allegedly—emphasis on the *allegedly*—used magic to disguise herself from a store owner while shoplifting about a thousand dollars in electronics. Then she was accused of using her magic to convince the judge she was innocent despite evidence to the contrary."

Drew's brows appeared over the tops of his sunglasses.

"Yeah, same. Though this looks less like she's a powerful magic user on the downlow and her ex, Melissa Mitchell, is actually framing Rebecca for her own thieving ways. The ex," I flipped the page over, "filed the claim about Rebecca's alleged powers. And the store owner also says he saw Melissa running from the shop. Plus, what a coincidence, she ended up with community service and probation for stealing."

"No offense, but I'm going to suggest to DuMarque that what they need on these trips isn't data analysts but some sort of mediator. Every one of these interviews is because of bad blood between the subject and whomever reported them."

I made a murmur of agreement. "Well, this third one isn't. Birdie Monroe. Though it's noted that the reporting agency could find no evidence of an actual person with that name, so they are listing it as an alias."

Drew nodded. "The only subject who turned themselves in for questioning. Like, ever."

"The weird part about this one is they never listed exactly *what* Birdie's thing is. Like Rebecca is allegedly a changeling, Cameron is allegedly a pyrokinetic...Birdie's form says 'bippity boppity boo, bitch,' and...that's it."

"Some people really want attention."

"There's easier ways. Get a face tattoo. Pierce something. Become a nudist but forget to tell your coworkers."

"Let's...put a pin in that last one," he said dryly. "We're here."

I tucked the files back into my satchel and gulped down the cold dregs of my coffee. "Alright. Let's get this over with."

Chapter Seven

DREW

Orrin was as amazing on the road as he'd been at the lab. When Cameron Diggs came in, visibly shaking and pale, staring at us like a spooked rabbit, Orrin managed, in just a few words, to soothe him and get him sitting in the admittedly uncomfortable conference room chair. By the end of our allotted hour, whenever my questions made Cameron startle and stammer, Orrin gently pried answers from him. He even got the blood sample, and a blushing, nervous Cameron let Orrin follow him to the bathroom to supervise the urine sample collection. By the time Cameron left, full of hotel-provided cookies and a bottle of lemonade Orrin bought him from the vending machine by the hotel pool, he no longer looked like he expected us to clap him in irons and drag him to the grand inquisitor.

"It's okay," Orrin said softly, giving him a squeeze on the shoulder. "You're going to be fine."

Cameron nodded, leaving with a weak smile but no longer shaking.

Rebecca was more difficult, but he worked his magic (so to speak) on her, too. She thought we were some ruse by her ex to frame her again or coerce her into admitting blame. "Heather's a bitch," she spat. "Her family's got more money than God, but she likes to steal shit and get away with it. They'd fucking buy her anything she wants. Hell, they could've made that stupid charge go away too, but she..." Rebecca sniffed once, hard. "She listened to her parents. I'm a bad influence, I'm poor, I'm weird, I'm ruining her life because I'm not going to college, and I just love her for her money." She rolled her eyes and slid down in her seat. "I lied to her a little. I told her my mom was psychic. She's not.

She's got one of those red hand places in the mall, but she's just great at cold reading. Heather believed me, though...bitch."

Orrin nodded, biting into one of the Hydrox cookies left on the tray. "Total bitch," he agreed.

Rebecca looked up, startled someone was agreeing with her, much less someone in a position to make her life hell. A small smile tipped her lips upward, and she relaxed a fraction.

After that, with Orrin rephrasing the questions into something friendlier, more palatable for her after I asked them as written, we teased out the responses we needed. The blood draw was harder, but Orrin distracted her with stories about the first time he got his nipple pierced (*hello, what?*) and she let him wait outside the bathroom while she took care of the other sample.

"That was hard," I sighed.

"I'm willing to bet neither of them pops positive at all." He stretched out across the conference room's inexplicably placed fake leather sofa. "Do we have time for lunch before Birdie Monroe?"

"About an hour."

"There's a sandwich shop across the street. I'll buy. What're you having?"

Go with him. It's almost a date if you're sitting together.

What the actual fuck, brain?

"Uh, tuna on rye if they have it. On white if they don't. No mustard but lots of pickles."

Grinning, he got to his feet. "You lost me at the tuna but won me back at the pickles. I'll be back in a few. Here." He tossed me some bills from his wallet. "Grab us some drinks from the machine, and we can eat in here before Birdie shows."

He left with a wave over his shoulder, whistling something under his breath.

"Ugh, I am so, so fucked," I groaned to myself. "He's even hotter in proximity."

THE VENDING MACHINE was one of the fancy kinds where you could use a card or bills and had to punch in the combination of letters and numbers for your choice on a digital keypad, which meant getting it to work took me forever.

Go figure. I worked with digital data all day, but an upscale vending machine eluded me.

"Fuck," I muttered. The soda I finally managed to select got wedged halfway down the clear chute leading to the retrieval slot.

"Here, let me." A young man with a shock of bright lavender hair shot through with dark blue streaks nudged me to one side and gently rocked the machine back and forth. After a moment, the bottle wobbled, then dropped to the slot. "Even these chi-chi ones respond to a little ultraviolence," he said, winking broadly.

Oh no...one of those guys.

"I suppose so." I nodded in dismissal. He didn't take the hint, watching while I paid for another bottle of soda and cheering when it fell straight to the bottom.

"Just had to threaten it a little." He stuck out a hand. "I haven't seen you before."

Automatically, I shook his hand without thinking. "Drew Hicks. I'm here for business."

He smiled. "I'm business. Birdie Monroe. I'd say it's nice to meet you, but I'm about to really fuck up your day."

ORRIN WAS LATE GETTING back, rushing in with a plastic bag of sandwiches, chips, and warm cookies, soaked to the skin. "Fucking tropical weather systems." He tossed the food onto the table. "How much time do we have left before the next interview?"

"Technically five minutes," Birdie answered before I could. "But I'm early. Oooooh, do I smell a Reuben? Nice!" He snatched the bag and rummaged through it, tossing the tuna sandwich to me and unwrapping Orrin's Rueben. He took a huge bite and grinned around the mouthful. "Sorry, I was gonna wait until my appointment time, but shit's happening, and we need to get a move on. Oh, hey, mind if I..."

He didn't wait for an answer, picking up Orrin's soda and cracking it open, downing a good third of it in a few gulps. "Shit, that's good. I'm so tired of the store-brand shit, you know? It tastes flat."

"Drew," Orrin said slowly. "What the actual fuck is happening?"

"I'm thinking it's a fever dream brought on by mold toxicity in an old hotel." I stared at Birdie as he polished off the Rueben and started in on one of the bags of chips, making happy noises.

"I'm prone to agree." Orrin frowned at Birdie. "He owes me lunch."

Looking up, Birdie grinned, crumpling the empty chip bag in one hand. "How 'bout I do you one better and save your ass before you can become an example? Both of you," he added, shooting me a wink. "We have about ten minutes before your office calls to say you need to head back ASAP and get ready for a meeting with the honchos."

"What?"

"Trust me." Birdie stood, took a few steps toward Orrin, and leaned forward at the waist until he was nearly whispering in Orrin's ear. "Jim wants to know if you remember the little rubber ball at the funeral home."

Orrin blanched, swaying on his feet until he could grab hold of the back of the chair in front of him. "You tell me what the fuck this is about," he hissed. "I'm not playing this game!"

"It's not a game. It's kind of the second act of a very long play, though, and we're not getting an intermission. Now." He clapped his hands. "I've been trying for months to get hold of you, Orrin. Jim finally pulled out the big guns and sent one of his messengers to talk to you on Saturday. They said they gave you the message." Pausing, he tilted his head like a curious, uncertain puppy. "They did, didn't they?"

"That fucking guy at the lab was a messenger?" I demanded, professionalism be damned. Orrin looked sick, his color a pasty, greenish hue that didn't bode well. I grabbed the unopened drink and moved to hold it against the back of his neck. "Here, cold things help with the wooziness."

"You're always buying me drinks," he chuckled weakly. "Though this isn't how I imagined it."

"You imagined me buying you drinks?"

Birdie whistled shrilly. "Boys, boys, boys. Focus. You can be all schmoopy later. Right now, there's a whole thing going on, and you need to pay attention. Jim doesn't trust just anyone to run messages for him. He didn't want to scare you." He softened his tone. "He thought if he did the whole," he pointed to his head and made a funny noise reminiscent of old '50s sci-fi style UFOs, "thing he does, you'd freak smooth out. Dude, I know Jace's a lot to take in, but you *fainted*?" He tsked. "That's kind of hard on a dude's ego."

"Jace?"

"Short, heavy coat. Teeth?" Birdie gestured to his mouth. "Did he give you the message or not?"

Orrin nodded, still sickly pale and visibly sweating. "I...he did."

"Good, good. Sometimes it's hard to tell whether Jace is actually passing on messages or not. Even someone as strong as Jim when it comes to Communicating can have a few misses now and then."

"What the Hell are you talking about?" My mouth finally worked, and my legs unlocked. I took the drink from my neck and pressed the cold bottle into Orrin's hands. "Here, sip this. You look bad."

"Thank you," he muttered dryly, opening the bottle to take a swig, glaring at Birdie. "How—"

"Wait for it." Birdie held up a finger.

Orrin's cell phone buzzed, then mine.

Orrin answered. "Hello? Yes, we're about to start our third interview now. Yes, he's already here. Mmmhmm. This evening? We'll be back well after close of business due to traffic." He paused, darting a glance up at me. "I see. Of course. Of course. We'll be there. I'll tell him to check his messages."

Birdie's smile was slow and sharp. "Jim says he can help. But you have to come with me now." He fixed Orrin with a steady stare. "Well?"

Orrin licked his lips, staring hard at Birdie. "If Jim is telling the truth, he can tell me his real name."

Birdie smiled benevolently. "That *is* his real name, like Birdie's mine." He paused, frowned, and sighed. "Fine, fine. Jim says—"

"Jim says," I interrupted. "Look, unless you've got a mouse in your pocket or a bug in your ear, Jim's not saying anything to you right now. Jim—"

Orrin's face was so pale I could make out the blue veins in his eyelids. He was staring past me, at the whiteboard running along one wall. The green marker moved around chest-height, letters appearing along the surface.

Hi, Orrin. Long time no see.

Pardon the bad joke.

"IS HE OKAY?"

I did not faint.

I just...sat down on the floor suddenly and closed my eyes.

"I think so."

I opened my eyes. Orrin was leaning over me, still green around the gills, and Birdie hovered over his shoulder, looking way too amused. "I—"

"Shhh, don't speak. What we have is too special to be ruined by mere words," Birdie urged dramatically. "Now, to answer your questions: No, he's not a ghost. Yes, he's a real person. No, I didn't do that.

And yes, we need to get the fuck out of here *now*. Shhhh," he added when I started to speak, "*now*. Come with me if you want to live."

"Your accent is terrible," Orrin said weakly.

"Nah, it's great. Arnold's the one who does it wrong. Come on. They're already on to you two, so we have like zero time to get on the road and get back. I wouldn't be surprised if they tossed your place already, Or."

"Or?" I made a face. "Or?"

"Hey, it's his name. He can tell me if he doesn't like it."

Orrin shook his head. "I hate it."

"Hmph. No taste. Come on. Jim, see you at the house? Well...*see* in the colloquial." He paused and snorted. "I know, I know. Okay. One two three, break."

"No." I rested my hip on the conference table and folded my arms across my chest. "This isn't some game, Mr. Monroe. If you don't want to answer questions, fine. We can't force you...though HEEL can compel you to speak with a representative from the Department of Human Developmental Studies."

As if scared, Birdie held up his hands and said in a faux-frightened voice, "Oh, no, the Feds! Oh, hey," he dropped his hands and slipped into a more normal tone, "do you think Fox Mulder will be there? Because I'm pretty sure he could *compel* me to do a lot of things."

Orrin edged closer to me. "Drew, one of us needs to call and find out why they want us back so soon. I have a feeling—"

I nodded. "You call. I'm going to talk to your new friend Birdie."

Orrin's brows crept up. "For the record, I know you were trying to sound threatening and tough, but that just came out sounding kind of creepy and wrong."

Birdie grinned. "Either way, I'm down."

Orrin snorted softly. "I'm stepping out into the hall."

"Don't go far," Birdie and I said at the same time. I glared at him. "Don't," I said sharply, "you dare call jinx."

"I wouldn't dream of it," he purred. "Okay, now that Or's gone, ask me your questions." He hopped up to sit on the table and let his legs swing, childlike even though his tense posture and sharp gaze were anything but.

"You already know what I want to ask."

He shrugged. "Maybe I just want to hear the melodious sound of your mellifluous voice."

My glare was clearly working overtime because he threw up his hands and dropped the Puckish demeanor. "Fine," he sighed. "Your buddy's been set up. That bloodwork he had on Saturday popped positive for indicators."

I didn't have to ask what indicators. "That's impossible. Orrin's been tested regularly since infancy. He's not magical."

"Okay, I hear you, but let me run something past you. What if he was?" Birdie's eyes went wide, and he mimed an explosion with his hands. "That'd be something, huh?"

"Even if it was true, how the Hell would you know?" I demanded. "The lab's database is beyond secure—I'd know since I helped encrypt it."

Birdie snorted. "He popped a positive, my dude. You know what that means—all positives get sent automatically to the Department of Human Developmental Research database. Then HEEL is notified." He made a face. "And someone at HEEL *really* wants Orrin to feel bad for lying about his status."

"You didn't answer my other question," I pointed out even as my mind reeled, pulled in a dozen directions at once. Was Orrin getting fired? What did this mean for the project? *Why had he lied*? Or was this some colossal fuckup, one of the exceedingly rare cases of a misread on the test?

"If HEEL is notified, all labs are notified, since all the labs working on magical lineage revivals and restoration are linked in to the DHDS' databases." Birdie slid from the table and patted me on the chest, moving to hold open the door for Orrin as he returned. "You—well, Orrin—has friends in...well, not really *high* places so much as well-placed places." He winked. "So, ready to go? Because trust me, we don't have a lot of time. They're gonna send someone to bring you back if you don't get a move on."

Orrin screwed up his face, something between a grimace and a snarl. "I couldn't get anyone other than Linda to pick up, and all she said was it was quiet at the front desk."

Birdie made an impatient noise. I ignored him. I opened my mouth to say we should cut Birdie loose, have hotel security escort him off-premises, maybe even call the local police, but Orrin cut me off. "Birdie, how did you know about the rubber ball?"

"Jim told me." He shrugged. "I was only told he played catch with you at your father's funeral, and he said to remind you of the rubber ball. You'd know."

Orrin nodded slowly. "And Jim..."

"Jim's Jim. And I'm not kidding when I said we need to shake a leg here, y'all. I can promise you DuMarque has his knickers in a hell of a knot already. He's gonna call the local DHDS field office to escort you in for questioning."

"Shit," Orrin muttered. "Why?"

"They think you lied about your lineage status," I said. "The bloodwork from Saturday showed indicators."

He made a face at me, this one incredulous. "Bullshit. I'm as magical as a paper bag."

Glancing at his phone, Birdie muttered a string of fluent profanities. "Look, we've got five minutes, okay? There's movement on the local channels, and I'd bet my last clean pair of socks it's about you two. So, either wait here to see for yourself, or take a leap of faith and let's head back to Houston to face the lion in his den."

"And then what?" I asked at the same time Orrin demanded, "And why are you coming?"

Birdie's smile was beatific. "Because. I need a ride back home, and I'll be damned if I'm hitching again."

ORRIN REMEMBERED TO grab our suitcases. We didn't even stop to check out. Birdie bustled us past the front desk and out into the post-storm humidity that made it hard to breathe and everything feel disgusting. Not bothering to be neat this time, we tossed our bags in the back, and Birdie climbed into the bench seat.

Orrin shot me a wide-eyed look. "This has become the weirdest day of my life, and I say that as someone who once did a naked run through downtown Seattle on a bet."

"Well, Seattle." Birdie shrugged. "They do Bumbershoot there, and people ride bikes naked. No big deal." He paused, leaning forward to glance at Orrin's lap. "Well, maybe a slightly bigger than average deal."

"Hey!"

"Sorry, sorry. Trying to lighten the mood. Now, we got off on a weird foot, didn't we? Okay, I'm Birdie. Hi. I work with Jim and Halloran—"

"Halloran?"

"Big bad Halloran. He says hi, too, but he's pretty sure you wouldn't remember him. The last time he saw you was your dad's funeral, but you didn't see him."

Groaning, Orrin let his head hang down, resting his weight against the seatbelt. "What the fuck is my life?"

Birdie patted us both on the shoulder and sat back. "We're getting to that. But first, most important question of the day: do you have any books at your place? It's a long shot, but I figured I'd start with the point-blank questions."

"Er..." Orrin shot me a startled gaze. "I... yes?"

"Good, good. Now, did any of them come from your dad, by any chance?"

"What? I have some comic books we bought together when I was little, and I have his baby book my grandma made when he was tiny."

Birdie made a disappointed sound. "But not, like...an ancient text or something? Maybe a scroll?" He whistled through his teeth, wiggling his brows at me in a sort of *hint hint hint* expression. "Maybe, oh, I don't know... A codex?" His gaze sharpened and tone shifted to something more serious. "Some old and venerable tome handed down through the ages, imparting wisdom an all the little Grimm children? Secrets of the ages, the history of magical lineages from ages past?"

"Oh, you mean this?" Orrin reached into his satchel, then brought his hand back out, middle finger extended. "It's a family heirloom."

Birdie stared at him. "You," he said finally. "I like you. But no, seriously though, you don't happen to just have that, do you? I checked the local libraries but nada. And it's not exactly floating around on Google, you know? So if you happen to have it..."

"So, should I just drive straight to the nearest cop shop, or are we going for a mental health check first?"

Orrin opened his mouth, but Birdie was faster. "If you want to know what's up, keep driving." He tapped Orrin on the shoulder. "If you'd just answered your damned texts this morning, we wouldn't be here right now."

"That was you?" Orrin whipped around in his seat as far as the belt would let him.

"Well, Jim, technically. Jim Reynard."

"Halloran and Reynard," I murmured. "What, is he, like, stalking Orrin or something? I know corporate headhunting is a thing, but isn't this illegal territory?"

"He's not stalking him, dingus—he's keeping an eye on him. He promised your dad, Orrin." All the lilting bravado dropped from Birdie's voice. When he wasn't putting on a show, he was a soft tenor with the barest trace of a Southern accent. Or maybe that was an act, too.

Orrin, who had been looking a little softer, tensed right back up. "Nope. Bullshit. My father would never have asked his ex-fucking-boss to 'keep an eye on me.'"

With a thoughtful humming noise, Birdie sat back in his seat. "You're going to have a very long day." He kept his mouth shut for the rest of the drive back to Houston.

Chapter Eight

ORRIN

"What the hell are we doing?" I muttered. Birdie was still in the back of Drew's Forester, eyes closed and sitting still, but he wasn't asleep. It was just a feeling, like he was waiting and listening instead of actually resting. "Are we going to be accused of kidnapping him or something?"

"More likely they'd accuse him." Drew pulled his car into his employee parking spot. "He's the one who dragged us out of the hotel and got in my car, isn't he?"

"But we're the jerks who let him." I glanced back. "Is he gonna steal your car if we leave him here? We can't take him in with us. It's after hours."

Traffic had been the beast we'd fully expected. Part of me mourned the opportunity to spend a night in a hotel with Drew. And even if it was Beaumont fucking Texas and not somewhere romantic or sexy. Or...just not Beaumont. Though logic reminded me we had separate rooms booked, my fanciful thoughts invented all sorts of scenarios to force us to share a room and hopefully a bed.

I glanced at Drew as he studied Birdie in the rearview mirror. *Ugh*. He was still so hot, and so fucking competent and smart, and I'd bet he could do amazing things with those long fingers of his...

Drew cleared his throat. I realized, belatedly, he had shifted his attention to me. I had no idea how long he'd been staring at me, staring at him. "Um."

"See something you like?" Birdie asked from the back seat, eyes still closed. "Don't lie; I'll know."

"You are giving me a headache," Drew declared. "If we come out, and my car's gone, I'll find you. Got me?"

Birdie opened one eye and grinned. "You can't get rid of me so easily. Just remember what Jim said, Orrin." He opened his other eye and, quick as a cat, pressed his face practically against mine. "Run."

"I ALREADY TOLD YOU the first three times you asked—I don't know what the fuck we're doing," Drew muttered as we took the lift up to the sixth floor, where DuMarque had instructed us to meet him in the conference room. The conference room on six was intimidating, one of those old-school oak-paneled jobs you expected to get fired in.

Which, given how things were going, was likely what was about to happen.

"We literally just started this project," I muttered. "How could they kick us out this fast?"

"Hey, slow down there. Who said we're getting fired? Birdie? Why the hell are you believing him? He's a stranger to us."

I hesitated. He was an absolute stranger...but he knew Jim. Or knew about Jim. And how could he? I barely remembered the story happening to me. If I thought hard about it, I could see the fuzzy details, like watching an old sitcom on a janky TV. The only part of that day that really stood out for me was my dad in the coffin. Figuring out finally he wasn't coming back, ever. Jim was...nebulous. I didn't even associate him with Reynard, as someone my parents had worked with, until Birdie said his surname. In my head, Jim was suit-clad legs and a vague, sad smile, holding up a ball.

Not someone I associated with James Reynard, former lead researcher with HEEL, who fell from public grace when he and one of the other lead researchers split from the company. But the fact Birdie knew at least enough to mention that private moment decades ago between a scared, confused little boy and a man he never saw again? That fuzzy fizzy watermelon feeling was back and making me feel like not believing Birdie would lead to some very bad things.

"He knew about a moment there's no way he could have unless Jim or I told him," I finally said as the elevator doors slid open on six. "And since I never met Birdie before today, the only person who could have told him is Jim."

"Jim of the levitating markers," Drew said quietly, discomfort heavy in his words.

"That...okay, that was fucked up," I acknowledged as we reached the closed conference room doors. "But there's so many ways that could have happened. Hello, magic?" I pushed open the door, and we both froze. Seated along one side of the table was DuMarque, Ivan, a woman I recognized but didn't know by name, and Benny, who looked incredibly uncomfortable.

"Hey," Benny muttered, ducking his face when DuMarque sent him a quelling, acid glare.

"Gentlemen. Please be seated. Have you dropped the samples at the lab from today?"

Drew nodded. "Yes, Doctor DuMarque. On the way up here. Left them in the secure unit to be tested tomorrow."

DuMarque nodded. "Good. Well, we have some interesting news, don't we?"

Benny winced. "I'm sorry," he said miserably.

Ivan grinned. "Orrin, my man...you are a slick one, aren't you? Very slick." He elbowed the woman. "Mina, you didn't tell me how slick Orrin was."

"How the hell would I know?" she groused. "I am literally just meeting him right now."

Drew frowned. "Mina, what's going on? Why are you even up here?" He glanced at me. "She works in IT with me. She's actually co-lead on a few projects with me, too."

"Not anymore," DuMarque sighed. "Mina will be handling all of your projects for the time being. You're suspended pending investigation, Mr. Hicks. And you..." He turned his sharp gaze to me. "You took this position under false pretenses. The blood sample you gave Benny on Saturday came back positive today, Orrin." He sighed sadly, rising to his full height and leaning over the table to pin me with his hard eyes. "You're such an intelligent man, Orrin, but book smarts don't always translate to common sense." DuMarque clicked his tongue disapprovingly. "There's no other way you could have tested positive for the markers, not after years of unequivocally negative tests. You're fired, Orrin, and you're officially under investigation by the Department of Enhanced Human Security regarding the theft of Revive serum from this lab."

"I CAN'T BELIEVE THEY didn't let me keep my ficus."

"To be fair, you kind of stole the ficus in the first place."

"You knew?" I rolled my head to one side and staring up at Drew, perched stiffly on my beloved Queen Anne chair. "You didn't even know me when I liberated Bitey from the lobby."

"I remembered there had been three ficus. Then one day there were two, and I saw a ficus being wrestled onto the elevator. I'm not a genius, but I can connect those dots," Drew said with a soft smile.

Drew had driven us back to my apartment, and we trooped in quietly, Birdie not deigning to say he told us so, Drew fuming, and me in shock. Birdie was rambling around my loft, on the phone with someone who apparently only required grunted, nonverbal responses. Drew had already called a lawyer friend of his to see what could be done, and I...didn't.

The only lawyer I knew was a guy I met on Scruff, and I didn't think a mutual blowie in a club bathroom would mean I got free legal advice six months later.

Drew shifted, moving closer suddenly, and I found myself gathered in a surprise hug. "I'm sorry this is happening," he said roughly against my hair. "You don't deserve this."

"Neither do you," I pointed out, muffled by his chest. As the embrace continued, my heart did a funny triple time beat, and I found myself sinking into it, turning my face so my ear pressed over his heart. The smell of him—faint laundry soap, day-worn cologne, a bit of sweat, warm skin, the day's travel—flooded my senses as we sat, some strange bridge crossed without us trying. "Drew." I delighted in the small shiver racing through him and against me. "I'm not sure how you're meaning this. Like is it a 'you feel bad for me' hug or a 'you're attracted to me, but you're bad at flirting' hug or..."

"Oh, my God," he groaned, but didn't let go. "The second one," he admitted. "I'm just...really bad at peopling. Like, tremendously bad at it. And I was feeling brave, so..." He started to let go, but I clung harder.

"Oh, no you don't. I've had the hots for you for like two months now, so I'm leaning into this hug in case you come to your senses later and realize you're just feeling touchy after a shitty day."

Drew laughed softly and started to say something else, but then his phone buzzed loud and long. "Shit. That's Brendon, my lawyer friend. Let me take this real quick." He disentangled himself from our embrace as he answered, gesturing toward the narrow balcony just off the main living area. I nodded, and he stepped out into the cool Houston evening, leaving me and Birdie inside.

Birdie had finished his own call, grinning at me from his seat on my kitchen bar. "So," he drawled. "You've had an interesting day..."

"Do you ever turn this off?" I waved a hand at him. "Or are you permanently stuck in Lost Boy mode?"

"Bangarang," he groaned, clasping his hand to his chest, "right in the heart!"

"Second star to the right and straight on to go fuck yourself." I shoved to my feet and strode toward my bedroom.

Halfway there, Birdie intercepted me. "Hey, okay, I'll drop the shit for now, alright? But you have your way of dealing with the world. I have mine. My world is a much shittier place when I have to not be Birdie Monroe. But you want some explainers, then I'll give them to you right now, you hear?"

I nodded, the sudden shift in his loud, lilting tone to the soft, Southern twang disorienting. "Start with you. Why were you one of our subjects today?"

"Because I told Jim there was no way you'd listen to him without someone to grab you by the shoulders and shake. And you'd need a native guide," he added with a flash of his showman grin. "Since I've been navigating these rapids since middle school, I'm the best weirdo for the job."

I shook my head. "I have no idea what half of that means, but okay. Jim...what the fuck is up with Jim?"

Birdie snickered. "I told him you'd say that, too. Jim's not a ghost, so don't worry. You know what they do at the lab, right? I mean, I know you know, but do you *know*? The Revive Project?"

"Of course. DuMarque, Halloran, and Reynard can trigger endocellular response in people from magical lines with weak or nonexistent response to stimuli. The serum kickstarts a reaction, allowing access to their latent abilities. It only works on magicals and can't create a magical person from a mundane."

His teeth flashed in another quick smile. "Very good. Top of the class. Now, do you know how they figured it out?"

"Years of post-doc work?"

"Cute. No, they needed guinea pigs, didn't they? Not the cute *reee reee reee* kind. The magical kind. The kind who would love to see their powers jacked up from E to Full."

"Okay..."

Birdie rolled his eyes, like he couldn't believe how slow on the uptake I was. "And Jim Reynard..." He made a rolling motion with one hand to say *go on*.

"Found test subjects?"

"*Was* a test subject! He Dr. Manhattaned himself!" Birdie snapped his fingers. "One minute he's chill and Jim and hanging out. The next, he's OD'd on Revive, and no one can fucking see him. Except he wears pants, as far as I know. I mean, no one has actually laid eyes on him in almost twenty years, though he swears he's not running around naked. But in addition to his little invisibility problem? Not only did Jim have a rarest-of-the-rare latent ability in his bloodline, matter transformation, he was also moderately gifted with telepathy and telekinesis."

"The marker..."

"Mmhmm. Jim's been using his woo-woo, Dr. Manhattan-with-pants powers to keep up with you for years, darling. He just hasn't had to let you know until recently." He winked. "You're not the only one he's keeping tabs on. He's known what DuMarque is up to forever, only he couldn't figure out how to stop him. But once he saw you were in the crosshairs..."

"Me? About my job?"

"Oh, you sweet summer child. I do wish I'd been born with telepathy because this bitch is exhausted, and it'd be so much easier to just think at you. Who do you think faked your blood test results up till this week? Sure, your parents managed that first one, but—"

"*What*?" I had to sit down. I had to call my mom. No, wait, I had to sit down more. "What the hell are you talking about?"

Birdie squatted down to face me, sitting on the floor. "DuMarque was obsessed with this codex thing, this book that'd been rumored to exist for centuries. It first popped up in the mid-Sixteenth century, and by then it'd already been in several hands, apparently. Different people over the decades added to it. Mostly scientists, in some form or another, but sometimes just laypeople or even clergy. The book has records of different types of magic over the centuries, how it appeared, how it changed..." He trailed off. "The last time anyone laid actual eyes on it was almost seventy years ago. It had come into the Grimm family sometime in the late eighteen hundreds, in England, and disappeared. DuMarque spent years of his life tracking it down, bribing and threatening and god knows what else. He found out it'd been in your family last, and that blew his lid, you know? He felt like it was some sort of sign. Your dad worked in the lab *and* was a descendent of the last person who had it in their hands." Birdie shook his head. My stomach was roiling with nausea, everything tilting off center and making me dizzy in my head.

"No," I said slowly. "No, my father would have said something if we had that lying around," I said on a shaky laugh. "Trust me, I'd have noticed if we had a big-ass ancient book sitting on the shelf next to the National Geographic issues and my Encyclopedia Brown series."

Birdie's smile was small and heartbreakingly kind. "Your dad must have known what was up. He wasn't naive, no matter how it can seem. He loved you and was afraid of DuMarque. Your dad asked Jim to make sure you stayed safe if anything ever happened to him." He laid one delicate hand on my shoulder and squeezed. "You've had your own invisible shadow for over a decade now, darling. Don't worry. He never peeks when you're naked. That'd be too weird."

THE CALL WITH MY MOTHER did not go well.She refused to answer me about Dad's death, denied ever finding me playing alone with a man named Jim at the funeral. "Don't you think that'd be something I'd have mentioned at least once over the years?" she demanded.

"I don't know. Maybe not. When would that even have come up? It's not like we talk about Dad's funeral a lot!" Or ever, really. It still hurt too much, for both of us.

"Orrin. I don't know what the Hell's gotten into you but this isn't funny. It's hurtful, and I'm worried that you're having some sort of breakdown or something."

"Wow. That's... That's nice of you, Mom. Ableist as fuck to boot."

She huffed a sigh, and silence stretched between us for a long, painful moment. "Orrin, I don't know how to respond here. You've had consistently negative tests for your entire life. I've seen them myself. And now you say you tested positive..." I could practically see her shaking her head, that disappointed look she got whenever I said something outlandish as a kid, the way she would just shake her head and *look* at me. I had a knee-jerk reflex to apologize and change the subject, but I swallowed it down. This wasn't me declaring I was going to go on *America's Got Talent* and quit college or shaving half my head because I got bored one summer.

I thought of my party trick. My fuzzy fizzy watermelon feeling.

I'd been able to do something for years, but it was a faint trickle of magic, nothing like the stronger abilities that had come before me. "Is it possible," I said carefully, "I mean even remotely, that there's been a mistake? That maybe those tests I took before were wrong?"

"Orrin, for god's sake," she snapped. "Why would I lie about any of this? Why do you always have to think there's something special about you, huh? You're perfectly mundane!"

Oh. There it was. "Mom, I'm not pulling this out of my ass here—"

"I loved your father," she ground out. "I loved that man beyond reason. But he..." She took a deep breath and let it out slowly, hissing air down the connection. "He made choices that led to his death. Choices that left me alone to take care of a little boy who *needed him, goddamnit!*" She sobbed, and I barely managed to swallow my own sound of dismay. "Your father always wanted to give you roots to protect you. He used to say that at least once a day to you, do you remember? Roots will protect you." She snorted softly. "He died because of something out of his control, Orrin. You tested negative because you tested negative. Any test after that—the ones you had for school, for work...think it through, baby. How could those have been manipulated? How?"

"Dr. Reynard—"

"Was discredited and hasn't had any meaningful work published in twenty years. He and Halloran left the lab to do their own thing and have gone nowhere," she said fiercely. "I don't know what's gotten into you, Orrin, but you need to hear me and hear me now. You are not special. You're not some faerie tale prince locked under an evil curse, waiting to be set free and return to your true family. You're mundane. I made sure, every test, that you were mundane. Your father died of stupidity, and anyone who tries to spin you a fancy tale about any of this is hurting you."

The buzz of the following silence was loud and made my ear hurt, but I couldn't set my phone down. If I did, it meant the call was over, and I wasn't going to get her to listen to me at all.

You're not special, Orrin.

That had been a common refrain in childhood—never said in cruel tones, but looking back as an adult, I could see the cruelty inherent in the words. Being raised mundane never bothered me, but whenever I asked questions about Dad, wanted to know more, see his videos, or talk to Grandma Luce about him, Mom had been quick to shut me down and remind me I wasn't like him. Remind me I was mundane. The call had ended soon after that, Mom informing me in cool tones that I needed to give serious thought to whatever nonsense I was going to spew, and she had to go get ready for a meeting with one of her numerous committees. I hung up and sat in the quiet room, suddenly exhausted and losing track of how much time had passed.

"Hey," Drew said softly. He stepped into my room where I'd gone to make the call, pulling the door closed behind him. "Birdie's sacked out on your couch. Snores like a bandsaw."

"It's always the little ones," I murmured.

Drew took the phone from my hand and started to put it on the charger.

"There's like a hundred texts from someone named Royce." He turned the screen to face me.

"I'll call him in the morning." I wanted to call him that very second, but it was already one a.m. He might have been a goer, but he did still have work in the morning.

"He seems worried. I'm not reading them, but that's a lot of texts..."

"He's my best friend," I sighed, and Drew seemed to relax. "Were you worried I had a boyfriend hidden away?" I teased.

"Maybe," he muttered. "Um, I'm guessing you don't have a spare bedroom or something?" He got to his feet, but I grabbed his wrist and tugged him back down to sit on the edge of the bed beside me. "Hello..."

"If I tell you I harbored a teeny-tiny fantasy about us having to share a bed at that hotel in Beaumont, and I was very disappointed we didn't get to, will you think poorly of me?"

"Think poorly of you? Are we Victorian now?"

"Just answer me," I laughed. "Is that too much to tell you this soon?"

He shook his head. "The thought...had crossed my mind, too."

"If I promise to be good and keep my hands above the covers and my knees crossed, would you stay in here with me tonight? It's been a really long day..."

He nodded. "I grok that."

"Grok? Ugh, he's hot and into classic sci-fi. Dear diary, today I met the man of my dreams." I mock-swooned back onto the bed.

"Dork," he huffed before getting up and heading for the bathroom.

The call with my mother hurt. Everything Birdie told me made my head ache. But at that very second, with every breath in my body, the only thing I wanted was Drew next to me, just next to me, so I could feel something good.

Chapter Nine

DREW

I usually slept naked, but I thought, for our first time—hopefully, not last time—sharing a bed, especially given the situation at hand, going commando might be a bit much.

After getting my toiletry bag from my overnight case, brushing my teeth, and giving my face a desultory wash, I headed back to Orrin's room to find him already deeply asleep. I shimmied down under the covers in my underpants after wondering, for a moment, if it would be better to sleep in my clean slacks instead. I finally gave up and crawled in beside him, carefully keeping to one side of the bed as he clung to the other like a sad koala.

I didn't know who he was talking to before I came in, but he'd looked gut-shot, curled up on the bed and sad-eyed, shaking as he held the phone to his ear. I had come to tell him Brendon, my lawyer friend, thought we might have a case against the lab, but he needed more information. We'd need to both talk to him. If Orrin thought I was going to leave him out to dry with this shit, he had another think coming.

Dozing off didn't take me long, even turning over the myriad thoughts in my brain. Before I knew it, the sun was glaring in my face, and Orrin was draped across me, his morning wood pressed firmly into my thigh.

"Morning," he muttered, arching just a little. "I'm dreaming, right? Because if I'm not, this is super awkward, and I'm going to have to go die of embarrassment."

"Don't do that," I murmured, voice raspy from hours of disuse. "I don't mind a bit. See, I've even got one of my own."

Eyes still closed, Orrin grinned. "If I'm dreaming, I can pretend today's not going to be a clusterfuck, and I get to spend it in bed with the hot guy I've been crushing on for months."

"What a coincidence. I'm having a dream where I get to be in bed with the hot guy I've been crushing on for months."

"We should introduce our hot guys to one another." Orrin stifled a small yawn as he wiggled even closer. "They might get along."

He moved his leg so it brushed against the hard length of my cock, making me moan softly. He hesitated, then did it again, pressing his lips to the side of my neck at the same time. A funny sensation bounced around in my head, through my veins and flooded my senses for a moment, bringing with it a feeling of *yes* and *right*. It wasn't magic but I knew without a doubt that something was meant to be...

"Good morning," he mumbled against my throat. "Tell me to stop if—"

"I'll tell you if it is."

He nodded, sliding his hand across my chest to give one of my nipples a good tweak. The heated pleasure shot straight to my cock, making it jump, trapped against my thigh. "Touch me. Anywhere. Please."

"Yes," I breathed, sliding my hands down his back, feeling the warm, soft texture of his skin and the shift of his muscles under my palms. I reached his ass, and he arched back into my hands. Chuckling, I gave the twin mounds a squeeze, making him groan against my chest and shift again, this time to straddle me. Still slumped over my body, he gave his hips thrust, making our cocks slide together through the layers of fabric. "Okay," I moaned. "Yes, okay..."

He nodded, pushing himself upright. And good God, did I love how he looked in the morning light. His wild halo of curls, free and untamed by the product he used to slick them down for work, was backlit by the rising sun. The light coming in through the window gilded him, his collarbones and navel making dark hollows, shifting and changing as he arched back. Tipping his face toward the ceiling, he braced himself against my thighs, starting a slow grind against my aching cock. Both of us moaned, for a moment forgetting Birdie existed and we weren't alone in the apartment.

"Fuck, Drew," he groaned, moving faster. Heat built in my belly, my balls tightening at the sensations spreading out between us. He was fucking beautiful to look at, to feel, and I forgot everything but him, everything but the two of us grinding together in the early morning light. As he panted my name, his eyes squeezed shut, nails biting into my chest. "Oh! Oh!" He pressed down hard, and sticky wet heat seeped through the fabric separating our cocks. "Oh," came out on a shuddered, soft breath as he gave another slow grind against me. "I want you to come, too," he murmured plaintively. "Come for me, Drew."

Like I needed the encouragement.

I grabbed onto his hips and rolled so I was on top. He giggled, wrapping his legs around my back and throwing his head back. I humped against him steadily, pressing, biting, kissing against his throat, his collarbones. When my release came, it was sudden and sharp. The gentle heat from before broke open like a dam, spilling lava through my veins as my orgasm shot from me.

Orrin gasped again, then made this throaty little growling noise, dirty and perfect as he wiggled his hips, spreading the mess between us. "Don't judge me," he scolded when I made a noise in the "ew" family. "Mess can be fun."

"I'll remind you of that next time." I patted around for anything to wipe us off and found nothing but bedding. "Shit. Let me go grab a towel or something."

Orrin unwrapped his legs from around me and sprawled out like a starfish. "I await your return," he called softly, grinning.

I made it to the bathroom and got myself cleaned up, grabbing one of the other hand towels to take back to Orrin. As I stepped out into the hall, a tall redhead shifted into my line of sight, both his brows raised. "Hey," he said slowly. "Quick question...what the fuck?"

"ROYCE," ORRIN GROANED, hastily cleaned and dressed in a pair of jeans so skinny I worried for his circulation, plus a t-shirt proclaiming *Mary's is for Lovers,* with a picture of a bearded drag queen on the front. Slumping over his kitchen bar, he slapped out with one hand until he found Royce's—the tall ginger—arm. "Please tell me you made coffee before you kept me from more morning lovin'."

"One, never use that phrase again. Two, of course I made coffee, you bitch. Here." He grabbed two mugs from the rack by the sink and headed for the automatic coffee maker. "I'm guessing you're Drew," he said to me. "I've heard a lot about you."

"Oh my God," Orrin muttered into his arms. "No..."

"Oh?" I asked. "Like..."

Grinning over his shoulder, Royce poured out the mugs and gestured to ask if I wanted one too. He added a third cup at my nod and grabbed the sugar bowl before carting everything over to the bar. "Oh, the usual. How competent you are. How sexy it is you were a mathlete."

"A what?"

"He wasn't a mathlete," Orrin muttered. "It was a math orgy."

"You read my alumni newsletter from like a decade ago? I feel stalked yet flattered." And oh, my God, if things with Orrin didn't work, I was going to ask Royce to marry me because he made a perfect cup of coffee.

Tousling Orrin's hair, Royce grinned. "So, you start talking now, or I swear to god I will go into all sorts of detail about Missy's next planned exhibit." He paused dramatically. "It involves nail clippings."

"Oh, sweet Jesus, no!" Orrin sat up. "I'll talk, I swear, officer!"

Birdie groaned from the sofa. "Are y'all done yet? I'm trying to get my beauty rest. The sexual tension in this place kept me up all night." He sat up, shoving his bright hair back out of his face, and froze. It was a split second, but it happened. He grinned, slow and feline, at Royce. "Hi, there. You're new."

"Down, boy," Orrin warned. "Royce, coffee, balcony, now."

Birdie watched the two of them head out with marked interest. "I like him. He can come with us."

"What the hell are you talking about?" I sipped my coffee and sighed. "I need to finish this cup before you get cryptic with me."

"Nothing to get cryptic about. Jim says we're going to have to get a move on. DuMarque's in a mood." Rolling his eyes, he flopped half-over the back of the couch to stare at me. "You're not gonna offer me any?"

"There's none left in the pot."

"There's a way to fix that."

Not wanting to be a dick just to be a dick, I got up and headed to make more coffee.

"Oh, this *is* good." I didn't have to look back to know Birdie'd just stolen my cup. "So, you're a mundane," he said as I filled the basket with fresh grounds. "What's that like?"

"Like...fine, I guess?"

"You didn't say normal. Nice. Most people would say it's normal."

"It's normal for me. Magic is normal for you."

"Very PC. You haven't even asked me what my party trick is."

"Do you want me to?" I turned to face him as the water percolated in the machine. "Or is this a test?"

"It can totally be both," he laughed. "You can't guess?" He wiggled his fingers at me.

"Nope."

"Spoilsport. Do you know what Touch is?"

The capital T was audible. After the last attempt to recodify terminology about forty years before, most magical abilities got grouped under umbrella terms. Touch encompassed anything needing physical contact with an object or person to affect them. Some telekinetics, for example, had to have some part of their body touching something to move it.

"Yeah. I pegged you more for a Manipulator, though." Manipulators could affect matter: making ice bubble away to steam in seconds, for example, or, in the case of some of the stronger ones, change the physical form of whatever they were touching. "Maybe a Charmer."

He let out a low whistle. "People are always underestimating Charmers. They don't realize how much power it takes to put magic into an object and sit there until it can be used later. More than I got." He polished off my—his, now—coffee. "Damn, that's good. Remind me to tell Royce he's a keeper."

"Birdie..."

"Fine, fine. Psychometry," he said in a cheesy gameshow narrator tone. "But I lucked out. Not only can I pull energy from something and get a read on it, I can throw energy right back into it. Well, if it's alive. For example, I got a nice hit of that post-coital vibe you got going on when I touched your mug. If I went outside right now, and I could convince him to stand still, I could give that to Royce and set his world on fire. Boom, jelly knees and sticky drawers."

"Ew."

Birdie shrugged. "It is what it is. And I learned the hard way how to turn it off when I have to. But Halloran...he figured out I could be helpful. He likes to give us strays jobs and—"

"Strays?"

"Keep up, okay? Halloran and Jim—Reynard, if you'd rather—broke off from HEEL because of DuMarque. They couldn't fight him on a fair field because he's got too many ties to powerful folks. Folks like your future brother-in-law, by the by, who is already hella-incensed you are even remotely tied to magic users. He's gonna love finding out about Orrin," he added with a laugh.

"Vick can—" I closed my eyes and took a deep breath, then another. "Vick isn't my problem right now."

"You'd think," Birdie said cryptically. "Anyway. Strays. For ages, Halloran's known tons of us low-levels and unregistereds are floating around. A lot of us slipped through the testing cracks early on, or, in some cases, were pushed through the cracks as fast as their parents could manage. Not everyone wants their kiddos to grow up and use their witchy woo-woo powers to help the Department of Human Developmental Studies or some shit." He reached past me and snagged a banana from the fruit bowl. "So, Halloran has a safe space for us. Well, a few actually. He finds us living situations with others like us or allies. He can get fake IDs if needed and basically help us start over."

Oh... "Do you happen to know a young woman named Sarah?" I knew affecting nonchalance was useless. "She has a daughter..."

Birdie quirked a brow. "Now, now. That's confidential," he said softly. "But if I knew of someone like her, they wouldn't be the first or last we found, looking for a safer life for themselves and their kid. And they wouldn't be the first or last we set up safely."

"Wh—"

"Shhh." He pressed one of his blue-nailed fingers to my lips. "Confidential, sweet cheeks." He booped my nose none too gently. "But if I did know of someone named Sarah who had a daughter, and they recently were looking for somewhere safe to hole up, I would know they're well, and happy, and protected. Halloran makes sure anyone who needs it is set up alright."

"Is that why his lab's not doing well?" I asked. "He's funneling everything into a magical halfway house?"

Birdie snorted. "Not doing well...he's gonna love that. In fact," he pulled his phone out, "lemme tell him."

Birdie spun away, heading back into the den as he dialed. Both frowning deeply, Royce and Orrin slipped back in from the balcony. "What's wrong?" I gave in to the urge to pull Orrin into my arms as he drew near.

"DuMarque just pulled up outside. I saw him and Ivan getting out of the car. They didn't see us, but who looks up..."

Royce glanced back toward the windows. "Maybe they want to talk about the whole firing thing."

"Or maybe," Birdie announced, "we should go. Now. Is there an emergency exit?"

"At the end of the hall, yeah. It leads to an old fire escape that's been locked in place since like 1908, though."

"We'll have to chance it," Birdie said grimly. "Grab anything you need and let's go. Now."

Orrin stood in place, staring, wide-eyed at his loft. "But—"

"But we can come back for it," Birdie said gently. "Right now, Halloran is waiting for us. And Jim. Let's get going."

Chapter Ten

ORRIN

Royce refused to leave me. "I love you, you idiot. You've been my best friend since I knew what those words even meant. If something bad is happening, I'm coming with you, okay?"

He ended up sitting squished next to Birdie as we drove up 45 to what Birdie kept calling The Farmhouse. I could practically hear the capitalization. Every so often, we'd stop so Birdie could use his phone away from the car, and he'd direct us down some side road or country mile before getting back up on the freeway. After five hours, we bumped our way down a long, narrow dirt driveway in my poor little Beetle, rattling over chuckholes and stones until a massive farmhouse came into view. "Holy shit," I muttered. "This is where Halloran lives?"

"This is where he lives," Birdie confirmed. He pointed through the windshield at a massive structure in the distance, like a barn on steroids with wooden sides and a huge double door propped open. Inside, lights gleamed bright white, with silvery flickers of chrome. "And that's where he works. The lab."

"That..." Drew shook his head. "No, I've seen Halloran and Reynard's facility on a tour after post-grad. They have a place in Dallas and—"

"And that is their official story," Birdie said. "Come on. They're waiting on us."

We unpacked ourselves from my little car and stretched while Birdie bounded up the front steps of the farmhouse and threw open the dark wood door. Royce linked his fingers with mine, giving me a squeeze. "Hey, so, just an FYI... I might be unemployed later because I totally thought I'd be popping by your place to bug you before work, maybe bogart some coffee. I forgot to let Missy know I was running away from home with my bestie."

I snorted, the urge to laugh hysterically threatening to break free and treat us all to a cascade of my high-pitched giggles. "We can file for unemployment together. It'll be a bonding experience."

"Come on," Birdie shouted from inside the house. "I'm starving, and we can't eat till y'all sit your asses down!"

Drew moved to stand beside me and took my other hand.

"Fuck," I sighed. "Let's do this."

WALLACE J. HALLORAN looked less-than. In the videos from the old lab, in the pictures that sometimes popped up on the news, he looked hale and hearty, a tall scarecrow of a man radiating an air of healthy amusement at the world. Yet he still maintained a level of seriousness regarding magicals and the science around the Revive serum and its offshoots, making him seem less comical and more like a kindly uncle.

Which, if my father had lived, I supposed he might have been to me.

"Jim's resting," he announced as we edged into his foyer. "He's been overdoing it the past few days; he thinks he's superhuman or something." Halloran sighed, and the love was palpable. I could feel it wafting off him. Looking at him, I saw a certainty. He and Jim were forever. A brief, sharp laugh slipped out, and he turned to peer at me, sorrow and wonder flickering over his features. "You look so much like your dad. It was like seeing a ghost for a second there. I've glimpsed you from a distance and thought you had a resemblance, but up close? It's damn startling." He lifted his arm as if to hug me, then dropped it. "Well."

"Oh, hell," Birdie muttered. He shoved Halloran forward. "Hug him. You've been dying to do it for twenty years. Let's cut the maudlin.

I'm starving and swear to God, I will eat every burger in that kitchen on my own if I have to."

LUNCH STARTED STILTED and awkward and ended...well, stilted but less awkward. Royce and Birdie couldn't stop bickering. Once Halloran got over his case of the stares and started talking to me and Drew, we warmed to one another slowly. Birdie roped Drew into helping him and Royce clean up, so Halloran could slip away with me to his study, a spacious and distinctly comfortable room down the hall from the kitchen. Done entirely in pale pine and soft buttery yellows and creams, it was like stepping into a scoop of vanilla ice cream. I didn't realize I'd said that part out loud until Halloran barked a laugh. "Well, I do enjoy vanilla," he chuckled. "Ice cream, anyway."

I...ew. *No. Don't think about possible surrogate uncle sex.*

"Sit, sit. We need to talk." He pulled folders out of his file cabinet, arranging them on his desk with a practiced air. "I need you to try and understand—the things I'm telling you today are not meant to be an attack on your parents' choices, Orrin. But there's some things you need to know, and you should have been told years ago."

"Is it that I'm magical?" It was no use pretending I wasn't anymore. The fizzy feeling, the way I just *knew* things sometimes...my father. I couldn't deny it.

Halloran's lips twisted into a half-smirk. "Officially? No. But really? Yes." Taking his seat across the desk, he pushed one of the folders to me. "These are your actual medical records, including every blood test for the magic indicators you've had since you were born. The tests developed by HEEL are considered the gold standard. The ones from my lab," he added with a touch of smugness, "are better. Far more sensitive, require less blood, and detect a fine enough level to determine if your ability is latent or dominant. We're working on a test to determine *which* ability a child is born with, but that's not one of our front-burn-er projects. What we're most concerned with," he extracted another file from the pile, "is this."

The folder was full of names and test results. Some of them I recognized, like Sarah and Cameron and even Birdie (though his test was over a decade old and had his birth name marked through, Birdie Monroe written above it in pen). "What is this?"

"People, mostly young people, suspected of having magic but unregistered. DuMarque pushed registration under the guise of 'what's best for the magical community,'" he added with a grim twist to his expression. "It's nothing but a means to control."

"Why do you have this? Why would DuMarque..." I shook my head. "The project Drew and I were working on. It was interviewing people about these allegations, collecting samples."

"When I found out what DuMarque was having you do, I was sick." He took off his glasses and pinched the bridge of his nose. "DuMarque using you for this project is some contemptible revenge against your father, Orrin. Your dad tried to stop DuMarque from experimenting on people, on creating these ultra-high dose Revive magicals whose powers are just off the charts, and DuMarque killed him for it. When you started working for the lab, the ghost of the man who stopped him from reaching his goal sitting one floor below him? It was too tempting for DuMarque to ignore."

"So, he...he wanted me to help him find test subjects," I said carefully, making sure I understood, "to...to do what?"

"To create a killswitch," he said bluntly. "To determine the most efficacious method to kill someone with magic. To determine how to control all of you."

"Why?" The word was torn from my chest. "Why would they want to do that?"

"Control," he said quietly. "Always control. As magic fades, those who never had it fear those who do or who could." He shook his head. "No, not everyone." He shushed me before I could say the words myself. "But those in power... they fear the powerful. And even the most low-level magic is stronger than someone without a single drop of magic in their veins could be. At least, that's the way people like DuMarque think, and that's why he wants the killswitch."

"How can he even make something like that? There's so many magic users still in the world and so many abilities... They're not all the same. I mean, even with regular prescription drugs, they have to fiddle with formulations sometimes because some magic users have bad reactions."

Halloran tapped his finger aside his nose. "Got it in one. The serum is tailored to different magical abilities. What would kill a telekinetic wouldn't kill someone with the Sight, for example. The beauty—pardon my language—of the serum is it is not only untraceable, it doesn't damage the DNA itself."

"Oh, my God," I said, realization dawning. "They can harvest it from the bodies."

Halloran nodded, face grim. "When I left the lab, DuMarque was in the planning stages to create accelerators, serums to boost abilities to unthinkable levels. I'm sure that's what he has been working on, and that's why he's developed a killswitch. He needs living DNA, not the nanotech, to make these accelerators."

I STOPPED THROWING up my lunch long enough to throw myself into the soft bed Halloran had shown me to before lunch. I curled up on top of the comforter, staring at the wall and seeing nothing for I don't know how long, before I felt someone creep into bed behind me. "I'm not in the mood."

"I know," Royce murmured. "But I'm here anyway."

We lay like that for a long while, until the light from outside changed from bright gold-white to a mellow blue-purple as the sun dipped behind the trees. Finally, I turned to face him. Royce looked steadily at me, the tiny laugh lines by his eyes the only sign he wasn't the twelve-year-old boy who helped me practice kissing, the seven-year-old who hid under the bed with me during thunderstorms, the twenty-year-old who comforted me through my first big heartbreak while I held him through his.

"I'm glad you're the same," I said quietly. "You're the one thing that is."

He smiled. "I'm really not. I change all the time. So do you."

"Not like this." I lifted a finger to take in the house, the situation, everything around us. "This is too much."

"This is a lifetime of change in one abridged edition," he agreed. "But what can you do about it? Can you unknow whatever it was Halloran told you? Can you unlearn the things you learned?"

"No. And stop making sense."

"Sorry, I'm contractually obligated, as your best friend, to make sense at least once per week, and today's the day, you lucky dog."

"Can I ask for a raincheck? We could do the whole 'making sense' thing in, like, a month or so, when this all settles down?"

"Ah, Ori." He reached out to twirl some of my hair around his fingers, an old soothing gesture he began when we were in kindergarten and never really gave up. "Do you really think if you ignore it, it'll go away?"

"No," I said glumly. "It doesn't work for ex-boyfriends, and it won't work for this."

"There's a good boy." He laughed when I pinched his nipple in a not-fun way. "Okay, okay, you're a miserable shit and not a good boy. Better?"

"A little, yes."

We fell quiet again. Then he said, "Drew got a call from his sister. She's having some problems with the pregnancy, and Vick's out of town. He's heading to Houston in the morning for a bit."

"Ah."

"He's going to tell you later. Pretend I didn't blab."

"Why did you?"

He shrugged. "You know me. Can't keep a secret from you."

"Could you, though? If you had to?" I pushed up onto one elbow. "If you knew something that could hurt me or get me hurt, would you keep it from me?"

Royce stared at me. "No," he said. "I don't think I could."

I sank back down beside him and tangled my fingers with his. "That's why I love you, Royce."

"I thought it was for my sparkling wit and how amazing my ass looks in denim."

"That too."

"Orrin?" he said after another few minutes had passed. "Even if we'd known about your magic when we were kids, I'd still have been your best friend."

"Good," I said, squeezing his fingers again, "because I'd still be yours."

We were quiet together for a long time. I think we both drowsed a bit because I felt fuzzy and soft when I spoke again. "That thing I know now, because of Halloran... It could hurt a lot of people in the long run, if it happens."

Royce barely managed not to yawn in my face, turning his head at the last moment before opening his mouth for a jaw-cracking inhale. I feared for any small passing animals, lest they be sucked in. "And you think you need to fix it?"

I thought of what Halloran had told me. I thought of what it could mean for magic users.

I thought of my dad. He'd been dead for longer than I'd known him in life. He'd been dead longer than my mother had known him even. Years lost because of DuMarque, because of someone else's greed and fear.

Sarah and her little girl, others like her... they were out there, running from these rumors, knowing they weren't just scary stories told to people like them—like *us*. Knowing they were being hunted. Would Sarah live to see her little girl grow up, or would there be another kid out there who thought their parent died because of a mistake, some error in judgment, only to find out later they'd been murdered?

Certainty settled in my bones with a strange sort of calm. I was still afraid, but it wasn't shaking through me now. It was an awareness, an acknowledgment that what I was about to do was dangerous, and I might not survive or, if I did, I'd end up locked away for the rest of my life. But the knowledge that, if I succeeded, I'd at the very least slow DuMarque down and hopefully give Halloran and Jim and the others time to dismantle the rest of his work... It settled me.

I love you, Dad, and I'm sorry I ever thought you made a mistake.

"I think I have to," I said softly. "I don't think—"

"Stop," he said, pressing his fingers to my mouth. "There's always a choice, so don't say you don't have one."

"I don't think..." I said carefully, once he'd moved his hand back. "I don't think I could let anyone else do it. I feel like I owe it to my father."

"Your dad? Why?"

I closed my eyes again and ducked my head, pressing beneath his chin. "He died trying to make sure people like me and Birdie and Sarah and, hell, everyone, wouldn't be used up and thrown away, or worse. I need to do this for him, Royce."

Royce didn't say anything for a very long time. Then, finally, he sighed. "Goddammit, Ori. You're gonna get me in so much trouble." He was quiet again, his hand resting heavily on my shoulder. Finally, it slipped off, and he exhaled on a soft snore.

I waited another few minutes to be sure he was out, then rolled carefully out of bed. I was exhausted in ways I had never imagined before, but I wasn't sleepy. Not enough to make a good run at a nap anymore. Instead, I slipped my shoes on over my bare feet and slipped into the hallway. Drew and Birdie bickered about something in the den. The idea of trying to sneak past them and Halloran and god knows who else made my head ache. Though it gave me a tiny pang of guilt, I realized I just didn't want to be around anyone at the moment, not even Drew. Rather than approach them, I headed the other way down the corridor, toward what I thought was a door out onto the back porch, overlooking the now-overgrown field behind the house.

What I found when I pushed it open was a sort of library. IKEA bookshelves lined the walls, and more technical manuals and binders than I could easily count were stuffed on each level, most of them looking worse for wear in the glow of the desk lamp. An old, portable chalkboard with a wooden frame held together by duct tape stood against the window.

I hesitated, then shut the door behind me. I just needed some time alone, and this room was as good a place as any to hide away for a bit.

The only chair was the one behind an old metal desk, the kind I remembered my teachers having in middle school, probably older than all of the students put together. I settled into the creaky chair, the smell of old leather and book dust comforting and, suddenly, depressing. It reminded me of Dad, of his tiny office at home, of his beat-up VW Bug. Closing my eyes, I let my head fall back, a few tears leaking hot and sharp from the corners of my lids. My breath shuddered, and I nearly missed the soft clicking of chalk on slate under my exhale.

Sorry. I should've said something to let you know I was here.

Fuck.

I want to apologize for the hotel. That was needlessly dramatic.

A weak laugh bubbled up from my chest. "Well... Given the circumstances..."

You remind me so much of your dad. The pause was thoughtful, even though I couldn't see Jim's face to know for sure. I could *feel* him around me, his aura or whatever he wanted to call it. ***I know this is difficult to understand, but—***

"But," I interrupted, "Halloran told me about the killswitch and..." I made a vague gesture in the direction of the chalkboard. "You."

The pause was longer this time. A soft sigh, barely audible, rustled the silence. "It's difficult for me to speak aloud sometimes," Jim said quietly, the chalk tapping against the board. "Trying to send word to you via Jace..."

"Is he one of your, um... One of the people y'all are keeping safe?" I thought of Sarah, of Birdie, of who knew how many others. "Is he magical, too?"

"Yes. He's one of our first. He's been part of our program for quite a while, and his particular abilities make him well-suited to help me pass messages along."

"How so?"

Jim's voice was a little rough around the edges, lower than I thought it'd be, which made it more difficult to hear him when he spoke so quietly. "He's a telepath, a very receptive one." The chalk stopped tapping. "I wish I had approached you differently, Orrin. Sooner. Better."

"Yeah, same," I muttered. His chuckle was dry and warm. "I...I don't remember what you look like. Not really. And I'm sorry I don't. I remember you wore a suit to Dad's funeral. And the red ball."

With a rattle, a desk drawer was pulled open, and a small red ball, one of those high-bounce things sold in gumball machines at the grocery store, rose into the air, stopping about eye-height for me. "Your dad drove me nuts with this damn thing," he groused fondly. "The last time I saw him, we were sitting in my office, and he chucked it at me, joking about something. It rolled behind my file cabinet. I told him I'd get the cleaners to pull the cabinet out for me. He, ah..."

I closed my eyes. The tears hurt like acid. "I wish I'd known you sooner, too. I wish—"

The chalkboard rattled. ***Your father would be proud of you. I don't have to tell you that. I know you know. But I feel like you need to re-***

member he'd be proud even if you told us all to fuck off today and never looked back.

I sniffed wetly, a horribly embarrassing honking noise. "If I told y'all to fuck off, I'd be letting him down."

Maybe, he wrote slowly, like he was considering each word before committing. ***But you'd be true to yourself. If that was what you wanted to do, at least. Is it?***

I didn't have to think, not with that familiar fizzy-watermelon buzz in my veins and the absolute certainty settling in my bones. "No. No it's not."

The red ball bounced against the desk and hit me in the chest before landing in my lap. "Then," Jim said so softly I could barely hear him, "don't worry about disappointing him. Everything he did, he did because he loved *you*, not who he thought you should be. And he'd love you now, even if you were nothing like him." The door opened halfway, and I could feel the hesitation before he spoke again. "I need to get some rest before tomorrow, so I'll actually be useful. I recommend you do the same, Orrin."

I nodded. The door shut quietly, and I leaned back in the old chair again, clutching that red ball in my hand and thinking about someone I could barely remember, wondering what he'd do next.

Chapter Eleven

DREW

It was the asscrack of dawn when Birdie, Royce, Jim, and I left for Houston. Going into town, traffic wasn't too terrible until we neared the area where my sister lived, near the Galleria. The freeway there had been under construction for literally as long as I could remember, and I thought it might be some sort of faerie curse, if faeries were real. A perpetual mire of road cones and people who had no business driving on a busy freeway all leading to poorly marked exits, feeder roads where you had to take your life in your hands, and side streets, more asphalt patchwork than actual road. Yet people paid exorbitant sums to live in those neighborhoods, all because they were in the "right" part of town.

Royce and Birdie peeled off in the moving van with the intent of packing as much of Orrin's stuff up as they could before he lost the apartment. They offered to swing by my place and see what they could grab. I gave them a list of the few things I valued and couldn't replace, with plans to make some calls later in the day and arrange for the rest to be sold or put in storage.

Maybe Dee would want it when she found herself a safe place to land.

As it was, she was living in Vick's townhouse just off Westheimer, in an older neighborhood that had gone through a "tired" period in the late seventies but bloomed back to life during Houston's heyday in the eighties oil boom. The townhomes were all painted candy colors with wrought iron over the windows and neat, expensive yards. Looking at the rows of sameness gave me a headache.

When I knocked, Dee opened the door herself. "I gave Marla the week off." She shuffled aside to let me pass, wearing stretched-out sweats, a pair of hospital socks, and an old t-shirt I think had been mine at one point, tight over her rounded belly. "I'm pretty sure she was reporting back to Vick." She locked the door behind us. With a grunt, she pressed her hand to her belly and made a face, rocking back on her heels as she let out a low hiss of air.

"Are you okay?"

"No, I'm carrying the weight of a Buick on my bladder, and if I have a magic kid, my fiancé is threatening to accuse me of infidelity and force me to give her up for adoption," she spat, then clapped a hand over her mouth. "I wanted to ease into that. Sorry."

A hot calm washed over me. "Vick's in Austin? Just asking for a friend. Not because I'm going to drive there and kill him or anything."

"Drew, don't make this worse," she said in a low, tight tone. "Come on. I need to sit down before I fall down. And not one fucking word about my waddle."

I followed her through the short hall to the living room, helping her down the three steps into the sunken space and to the sofa, where she dropped down with a groan and sigh. I sat across from her and waited.

"Stop staring at me. It's freaking me out."

"There's the Dee I remember," I said with a soft laugh. "We haven't really talked in months, baby sister. I'm not counting those uncomfortable lunches with Vick in tow. And you called me for help. So I'm here. Let me help."

"I don't know what I was thinking," she admitted. "There's nothing you can do. Vick's... Vick. And I got myself into this, didn't I? It's because I wanted to be something I'm not and—"

"Stop." I moved to sit next to her; I couldn't loom there like I was Dad, staring down her bad choices. Not when she needed her brother. "No matter what decisions you made, no matter who you were trying to be, you don't deserve this, Dee. Your baby doesn't deserve this. If you're carrying a baby with magic ability—"

She scowled. "No one in our family's had magic since Great-great-grandma Ruth. And she was weak."

I nodded hesitantly. We all knew the family stories—Ruth immigrated to Louisiana from England in the late 1800's, one of a handful of mail-order spouses from weak and inconsistent magical lines. It had been a popular thing to do for families of a certain social standing in many countries. Even back then, magic had been growing weaker in some lines, not passing down to offspring consistently or at all. If you were wealthy and came from magical lineage, you tied yourself to other magical lines to keep things going.

Ruth had been the only one of six siblings to inherit any ability from their parents—family lore said she could see glimpses of the future. Our father insisted it was all bull, that she'd just been a girl eager to get out of a poor family, ready to marry her off to some local farmer before she was even twenty. I was prone to think Dad had been right, that she'd just been a girl wanting adventure and to get out of what she saw as a bad, or potentially bad, situation. Not a single one of Ruth's kids had been born with magic, and when they started testing kids at birth, not a single family member had shown a sign of the genetic markers indicating magical lineage.

SHE MOANED. "WHAT AM I going to do?"

I thought of Jim changing information for Orrin. Of Halloran and his connections everywhere. Of my baby sister, needing my help.

Of DuMarque, who wanted to track down magicals to make sure they were registered.

I thought of any kid I might have one day. What would I do for them?

"Let me help you, Dee. If that's what you want. If you say no, really no, I'll leave you alone, but know my door is always open, okay?"

She winced, pressing her hand against her belly again, and let out a long, low groan, her voice breaking at the end. When I reached for her, she waved me off. My hands fluttered uselessly as I tried to think of what to do, some way to comfort her, while she rocked forward and hunched over her belly. After a moment that felt like an hour, she let out a shuddering breath and pushed her hair back from her sweat-damp skin. "Shit, that was a big one."

"Um... when are you due?"

"Technically? Next week. Realistically? As soon as I can convince this little girl she wants out. I was going to just dangle a toy down there and, when she reaches out for it, grab her and pull, but I've been told that's medically impossible." She winced again. "Worth a shot, though, right?"

Dee was pale and sweating, her hands shaking as she pressed against the mound of her stomach.

"Okay, here's what we're about to do. What hospital are you supposed to go to?"

"What? No! Not today! I need to shower! I have hairy...everything! I can't go today!"

Still, she let me guide her to her feet. "Dee, I promise you, they don't care what is or is not groomed, and please never make me think of that again when it comes to you, okay? Let's go get you checked out. If it's nothing, you get to come home, okay?"

She hesitated, then nodded as another spasm wracked her body. "Fuck my life. Okay. Can I brush my teeth first?" She gasped, the next cramp right on top of the last. "Okay, screw that. Let's go."

YOU CAN ASK, YOU KNOW.

Jim's voice in my head startled me. I jumped in my seat, nearly waking Dee in her hospital bed. "I don't know what you mean."

Yes, you do. And you can think your reply. If you give me permission, I can—

"No thanks," I muttered. "That's a bridge too far for me right now."

I understand, he chuckled. How he managed a psychic chuckle, I'm not sure. ***As far as I know, I'm the only one in the world like this. Invisible, I mean. I'm pretty sure there's other middle-aged scientists who love a good IPA and are tragically basic in their music tastes.***

"What does this have to do with anything?"

Let me get to it. I'm the only one in the world like me. And rather than be angry or sad, I decided to use that to my advantage. So far, I've used it to help Orrin and people like Birdie. People like Halloran. Let me help your sister, Drew. Wallace can't get her into the private place until tomorrow, at the earliest. She needs someone on watch here until then at least.

"You barely know me." I watched my sister shift in her sleep. It had been a false alarm, but her blood pressure was so high they decided to keep her for observation anyway. Already, a few people claiming to be "dear friends" had tried to stop by and see her, backing off only when I firmly informed the staff she was to have no visitors.

I was sure that would hit the gossip sites before midnight, and Vick would be thrilled.

I'll stay outside the room, Jim continued. ***She'll literally never know I'm here.***

"What if something happens, and she needs to know?"

Then we burn that bridge when we come to it, he replied blithely.

Oh, Christ...

I heard that.

BIRDIE AND ROYCE MET me at the hospital. "Jim's staying here a day or two," I announced. "He said he'll let us know when he needs to be picked up."

Royce looked momentarily confused. "Jim...was with us in the car? I'm not sure how I feel about not knowing someone was there."

"He rode with me," I pointed out.

"Oh. Okay then." He hopped up into the moving van. "Are you sure you didn't want anything else? It was, like...four boxes and a bag."

"I'm sure," I promised. "It's time for me to start over. Start living as me."

Snorting, Birdie gave me a knowing look. "Get your ass in the car, Drew. You're sounding like an after-school special or something. Let's get home and see what Orrin's gotten himself into. Halloran was going to drop some more doozies on him today."

Suddenly, my need to see Orrin surged back into place. All day, it'd been simmering underneath my need to protect Dee, my worries for her and my yet-to-be-born niece. But now, knowing they were safe, even if it was in a way I'd never dreamed of, every part of me was anxious to get back to the farmhouse and see Orrin. "Alright, let's go. We're not stopping at Bucc-ees," I added.

"Speak for yourself," Birdie called. Before they pulled away, I could already hear the bass thump of whatever he'd set on the stereo and Royce's shrill cry of displeasure.

How did my life get like this so fast? And why had I let it wait so long...

"7-11 ISN'T THE SAME as Bucc-ees," Royce pointed out at our second stop of the trip.

"No, but we'd be back two hours sooner if we didn't have to keep stopping so y'all could compare the perfect slushies."

"It's science, my dude. And I got you something." Birdie tossed a copy of the *Dallas Morning Herald* into the open window of the SUV. "Looks like your old office is shut down."

Across the front page was a picture of HEEL with a smaller image of DuMarque as an inset. "'World-famous lab, researcher in magical science, shut down pending investigation by feds,'" I read. "What the..."

"Looks like someone called in about a dozen anonymous tips on everything from money laundering to improper storage of tissue samples." Birdie grinned a purple-toothed smile, reeking of grape slushy. "Damn shame the place is going to be nearly empty for at least a week."

"Birdie—"

Waving over his shoulder, he climbed into the van, arranging himself in the passenger seat. "Trust me. It'll be super helpful soon."

"For what?"

"Ask Orrin when we get back. Halloran's laying it on him right now. It's gonna be wild, man. So wild."

I pulled out of the parking lot, following the moving van back onto the highway. "I amend my previous thought," I said aloud to no one. "How did my life get like this, and why couldn't it have waited till I had my shit together?"

Chapter Twelve

ORRIN

"I don't think you've ever seen this before," Halloran murmured, setting a photo down in front of me. "I took it myself, before you were born," he said with a sad chuckle. "We felt immortal back then."

It was like being in a dream. But not a good one where everything was made of candy or something. One of those where you felt sick and the world wasn't right and you couldn't make it stop. Seeing my dad sitting in his office at home, the one I remembered him in, the one where I'd hid under his desk while he worked until he'd laugh and tug me out, swing me around. It came back in a flood of sense-memory. The smell of the room, his aftershave, the faint aroma of lunch cooking downstairs... I'd never seen this particular picture of my father before. It wasn't one of the publicity ones from the early days of the lab and definitely not one of the scads of candids my mother had hidden away in boxes in the hall closet, the ones I'd been slipping out over the years and taking to my place. "This is..." I shook my head. "He looks so young. Christ, is he in high school here?"

"He was about your age here. And that," he tapped a maroon book on the desk by Dad's elbow, "is the codex DuMarque is after, the one your father stole from him."

"Dad just...had it? The entire history of magic since Star Fall, and he kept it on his desk as a freaking paperweight?" I wanted to reach back through time and shake my father.

"It wasn't out on his desk all the time, but he certainly used it for research. I am fairly certain that was one of the reasons DuMarque used the killswitch serum. He knew your father had discovered DuMarque's line wasn't mundane at all."

Halloran placed another folder in front of me.

"The actual records. The ones I liberated from the lab before Jim and I left."

Inside, decades-old papers laid out the medical history of the DuMarques. Ivan tested positive at birth and again at every test thereafter. Though he was registered originally as pyrokinetic, the records in the official system listed him as mundane. "Your father wasn't the only one trying to hide tracks. But I'd say his reasoning was more...noble."

"He wasn't noble. He was scared."

"Sometimes, there's very little difference. Nobility, in this case, is being afraid but doing what must be done to ensure the wellbeing of another."

"Mom..."

"Your mother was afraid. Still is, I'm sure. When your father died, she knew who had killed him. There was no way she couldn't. When you got the job at the lab..." He trailed off. "Well. I can't say I am entirely supportive of her reasoning, but she figured, from what I could gather when we last spoke several years ago, that it was a case of 'better run with the devil than be in his path.' As long as you were working with DuMarque, she knew where he was in relation to you. And you were not *in* the lab, a potential guinea pig, because you, as far as everyone was concerned, were mundane."

Closing the folder, I let my head drop to my chest. "My entire life has been one long lie. I think I'm going to be sick." I pressed my face into my hands. "Everyone I've ever loved has lied to me, *about* me! Who the Hell would I be if I'd known?"

"Probably very much the same person." Halloran took my hands away from my face and passed me a tissue from the box on his desk. The lab in the barn was spacious and climate-controlled, but I felt closed in as I considered everything in front of me. My father's work on the codex tracing lineages, that ended up leading to his death. DuMarque and Ivan, both carrying strains of magic they'd increased with their use of Revive...

Jim, who was still there but not. Jim who was allegedly resting, since he'd used his magic so much over the past several days he could barely keep his eyes open.

I wondered briefly where he slept and how we would know. Did he have a room away from the house, or was one of us sharing accommodations with an invisible man?

"Stop thinking so hard; you'll blow a fuse," Halloran grouched. "Listen to me, Orrin Grimm, and pay attention because I'll say this one time and one time only. Your father never lied to you. He never kept things from you. He died before he could help guide you on the path you may have walked, and there's no going back to change that. You can't dwell in that haunted house, Orrin. You have to walk the path you're on and know he's with you." He pressed his hand against my chest, over my heart. "And yes, I know that was cheesy as hell, but give an old man a break."

"Old?" I laughed. "You're forty-eight."

"It's not the years—it's the mileage." He winked. "And yeah, I stole that line. Sue me."

"You and Birdie with the movie quotes," I huffed.

"Sometimes it's easier to use the words someone else has written, at least when it comes to other people."

"You sound like Drew. He says peopling is hard."

Halloran chuckled. "Peopling. I like that. And your Drew might be a kindred spirit of mine. Well. Enough of that. We know what we need to do, eh?"

"Eat lunch, save the world?"

"Eat lunch, *nap*, then save the world. Priorities, son. Priorities."

DREW RETURNED FROM his trip into Houston with a grim, gray expression on his face.

Royce and Birdie had packed up a lot of my apartment and worked down the list of things Drew had decided were most important in his place. All of us were vaguely horrified at his blithe claim the furniture was never to his liking anyway, so why not give it away? By the time they returned from the long trip south, Royce and Birdie were hopped up on Thirst Busters and a pound of beef jerky apiece.

Drew, though, was exhausted and nauseated from anxiety and not eating most of the day. I made us sandwiches from leftovers and poured glasses of sweet tea so we could have our late meal in the light of the stove's hood lamp.

"Dee's having a hard time," he said quietly as we stood, eating sandwiches over the kitchen sink. It was well past dinnertime by then, and I was peckish, but Drew was ravenous.

"Vick's figured out something is off. Test's not back yet, but Vick lied about his family being mundane. He's got a few relatives on his mom's side, apparently, with abilities. Not sure what, but Dee got an anonymous note the other day. Untraceable email. At least she says it is. She wouldn't let me check and see." He huffed a soft breath. "We had a relative several generations back who was apparently the last of her line to have magic, but..." He trailed off. "Well, we're finding out maybe things aren't always as latent as we think, huh?"

I grunted. "Chances are good y'all aren't carrying the gene anymore, though. And maybe the letter doesn't need tracing quite yet. It did its job, and anything else is just going to prolong her stay, isn't it?"

Sighing, he eyeballed the half of a sandwich still in his hand. "She had some funny pains today and was admitted to the hospital for observation. They're pretty sure it was false labor, but they're keeping her overnight."

"What about—"

"Vick's in Austin on some press junket for his senate run, but I was worried, too. Jim..." He trailed off, looking sheepish. "I left an invisible man guarding my sister's hospital room. I feel so weird saying that out loud." Drew rubbed the back of his neck, looking sheepish. "I know he was worn out but he said he could catch a nap there. I... Fucking hell, what is my life these days?"

I kissed him against the corner of his mouth. "You did the right thing, in my opinion. You love your sister, even though things have been rough between the two of you for a while. Protecting her and your niece? I promise you, Jim wouldn't have agreed to stay behind if he thought it was a bullshit request." A thought popping to life in my mind, I paused. "I think Halloran was trying to make a point earlier, and I thought it was crap, but now it kind of makes sense. But ugh, I still don't want to talk to my mother."

"Um, okay?"

I shook my head. "Don't worry about it yet. Finish your sandwich, though, because I have things to tell you that you need to sit down for."

TO BE FAIR, WHEN I got us settled on the sofa, I meant to simply tell Drew about what Halloran told me earlier, but it took us one blowjob apiece to get there. We were sprawled against one another, me over his chest, his leg hooked over mine, half-drowsy with our full stomachs and post-orgasm lassitude, when I remembered what I wanted to say. "Did you know DuMarque and Ivan are both magicals?"

"What?" He started to sit up, but I growled, and he fell back against the arm of the sofa. "How the Hell would I have known?"

"Sorry, just a conversational tic. And it flows better than 'you'll never believe what I fucking heard today.'"

"I don't know. That would've been less startling of a lead up."

"Hmm. Well, buckle up, baby cakes, because this is about to get wild."

Drew snickered, but before I was done, he shifted us both to sit up and stared at me, open-mouthed. "You are shitting me."

"Nope. It's all on hard copy to boot." I tapped the file folder Halloran had lent me, resting atop the banker's box of information he and Jim had gathered before, during, and after their time working with DuMarque. "There's so much in there about my parents I didn't know. Like the codex."

"The what now?"

"It's this collection of writings and research about magic—how and when it appeared in different regions, how people manifested it, early codifications of terminology and forays into the biology of magic users. Hell, there's even some super old school work with microscopy looking at the blood markers for magic. People have been adding to it for centuries, pretty much since the major Star Fall event happened up until the codex disappeared in the late 1800s. My father had it, and I kind of remember it but never saw inside it. He had a book he'd take with him sometimes when he left the house. I was so little, I don't..." I trailed off, shaking my head. "Halloran thinks it was passed to him from his father, who got it from his mother. Halloran and Jim suspect as much only because they remember my dad talking about it when they were developing Revive. He let them see pages of it, proud to be part of this line of researchers trying to learn about magic since the beginning."

"Your dad reminds me of you." Drew pulled me back against his chest. "You're not a scientist like he was, but the way you care so damned much." He brushed a kiss across the top of my head. "I wish I could've met him, but from how you and Royce talked about him earlier and the little I've heard Halloran and Jim say, I bet he'd be so proud of you."

I started to protest, but it lodged in my throat. I ended up sort of shaking my head, nodding, then letting out a shuddering breath. "Well, it gets worse. The Revive serum HEEL developed? It has an opposite number. A killswitch. DuMarque's been testing it on low-level magicals. That's why he's been having us see if any of these piddly reports bear fruit."

Drew made a horrified sound low in his throat, a sort of moaning sigh. "He's been...on humans?"

I nodded. "No one we've found. But there's been some..."

"And I'm guessing from the name, killswitch doesn't end in rainbows and puppies wearing onesies."

"No, but put a pin in that because I want to explore the possibility later." If you can't have dark humor in the face of possible murder, what can you have?

Oh, right...a healthy dose of fear and panic.

"Killswitch is like Revive but inverted in the effects. It does nothing to non-magicals other than maybe a bit of a headache, but for people with any magic? It's like setting off a time bomb in their body. Halloran doesn't know how far the experimentation has gone, just that it has been tested on some subjects who were later found dead of 'sudden, unexplained illnesses' or 'natural causes.' Most of them have been homeless or in precarious situations, so their deaths are unremarked on or poorly investigated." The headache brewing all day was finally making an official appearance, stage center, but I couldn't go to bed yet. "Come on, let's unpack this so you know what we're dealing with." I pulled the bank box closer.

Chapter Thirteen

DREW

"Walk me through this again."

"Revive," Orrin said, pointing to an empty vial, "enhances already present magical abilities, even if they are what you could call trace amounts. The problem is the dosage." He pointed to the other vial. "This is the killswitch, according to Jim. It's like the opposite of Revive. It..." He made a face, his lips pursing and his brows furrowing, eyes shining bright. "It's what killed my father."

"Shit, Orrin..." I pulled him against my side where we sat on the farmhouse's sofa. Halloran was in the lab across the property, but Birdie and Royce were still in the house, going through some piles of paperwork and trying to track down the codex. After Orrin's father's death, it was never found. Someone had trashed Orrin's home at least twice—robbed, his mother had said—but now he was fairly certain it was DuMarque's people looking for the codex.

Still staring at the vials, he leaned his head on my chest. "My mother always told me he died of a sudden illness, something like a stroke but not. And at his funeral, I remember Jim. It's fuzzy, but he played with me, asking me to move a ball. I was so mad at everyone for letting my father look wrong, for letting him lie in the weird bed and just not play with me." His fingers tangled themselves in the placket of my shirt. As he pressed his face closer against me, hot tears seeped through the fabric. "Knowing they murdered him? That DuMarque is who did it, and my mom... Fucking hell, why didn't she say anything to me? I fucking worked for the man who murdered my father, Drew, and she never said a goddamned word!"

"I think," I said slowly, "she might have been scared." He made a disgusted noise, low in his throat. "I don't know, baby. I really don't understand how she could have let it happen. But I also know I've never been in that position myself."

"I would like to think if you ever spawned a creation and claimed to love it, you wouldn't lie to it about everything and then blithely congratulate it on working with its other parent's killer."

"I also wouldn't call my child an 'it,' so..."

Orrin blew a raspberry at me.

"So what do you want to do?" I asked after a long, comfortable silence. "Report the lab? It's already temporarily closed for investigation, thanks to Vick."

Orrin snorted softly. "I'm sure you're loving how your future brother-in-law's actually helping."

"He's not doing it on purpose. He thinks he's sticking it to magicals and preventing the, in his words, 'proliferation of adulterated human genomes into the population.'"

"Methinks he doth protest too much. Methinks he has some adulterated genomes of his own, to be so afraid."

"Seriously? And methinks?"

He smiled against me. "I was stuck on a roll. It won't happen again. And we already know Ivan and DuMarque have been lying about their abilities for ages so they can avoid being monitored by the DHDS. What's to stop Vick from lying, too?"

"Vick doesn't have the resources to cover his trail," I reminded him. "He doesn't have an insider at a lab to doctor his blood work. He also comes from a long line of mundanes."

"As far as you know," he countered. "For all we know, Vick's lying. It wouldn't be the first time someone like him has lied about their background in order to be more appealing to their audience."

I acknowledged his veracity with a grunt.

Orrin climbed onto my lap and draped his arms around my neck. "Besides, you're not too far off the mark. I do want to expose the lab. But I'm not calling the authorities on them."

"Wait, what? No, Orrin—" I began, but he pressed a hard, fast kiss to my lips, silencing me.

"I'll talk to Jim first, see if he can do it for us."

I groaned under my breath. Jim freaked me out. I knew now when he was nearby—he went to great lengths to make sound as he walked, wear a splash of aftershave or something, give us a sign of his presence—but I couldn't get past how he spoke to us using his thoughts alone or how he could reach out so far and manipulate things as he wanted.

"Orrin, let's think of something more concrete, okay? Something not involving breaking and entering."

He kissed me again. "Let me talk to Jim, and we'll go from there."

TALKING TO JIM ENDED up in a drive to Houston. "We're staying in a hotel," a disembodied voice from the back of the rental van announced. "Just to be on the safe side. I'm fairly certain both of y'all's apartments are being watched."

"I'm about to lose my apartment," Orrin muttered. "They can watch it all they like so long as I can get my keepsakes out first."

I steered the van into the small hotel parking lot, Royce and Birdie pulling up beside us in a rented SUV. There were too many of us to fit into Orrin's Beetle again. Though Halloran had arranged to retrieve my car from in front of Orrin's apartment a few days before, we didn't feel safe driving it back into town.

So we rented the only two vehicles available on short notice in Micklethwaite, Texas: an eighteen-foot moving van and an SUV that smelled like a cheese sandwich died inside somewhere.

I jogged inside and paid for our room, moving the van around to the other side of the hotel to park directly in front of the door. Royce and Birdie tumbled out of the SUV, scowling. "If this place has weird stains on the bed," Royce warned, "I'm sleeping in the car."

"Same," Birdie and Orrin muttered at the same time.

"It's just for the night." I unlocked the door with the grungy plastic keycard the desk clerk handed over. We crowded into the door, hit full in the face by that cold air hotel smell of disinfectant and dusty carpet. An invisible hand grasped my elbow, and, in my head, I heard the words, ***I hope this room comes with complimentary antibiotics.***

ORRIN COULDN'T SIT still. He popped up and down like popcorn, pacing and fidgeting as it got darker.

"We're not going tonight," Royce sighed. "Remember the plan."

"I like my plan better," Orrin muttered. I felt more than heard Jim chuckle. As it stood, the plan was for Jim to make contact with DuMarque in the morning and basically put the fear of the powers that be into him. And, if fear tactics didn't work, Birdie was on hand to do a little light-fingered evidence collecting. Neither of them could talk Orrin out of going, and if Orrin was going, I was at his side.

"Have you called your mom?" Birdie asked suddenly. "Maybe to check in, let her know what's going on?"

"You are weirdly invested in my relationship with my mother," Orrin snapped. "And I haven't spoken to her since that night in my loft. If she wants to keep lying to me, I don't have to hear it."

Birdie nodded, his expression a bit sad. "I don't know, man. Your dad was real big on making sure you had roots to protect you."

"Why the Hell does everyone keep bringing that up?" he growled. "He didn't say it about me, anyway. He said, 'we need roots to keep us safe.' Not the other thing. It's what he's saying on that damned hologram in the lobby. God knows I've listened to it a thousand times; I have it memorized." He scrubbed his hands over his face and growled again, inarticulate and full of annoyance. "This is going to end badly. I know it is. I Know."

I heard the emphasis. Not just knew. He Knew.

He turned to me, almost desperately grabbing for my hands. "Drew, come on. We can get in and get out."

"How? Our security cards aren't good anymore. And you think the night guard is going to let us waltz in while the place is on lockdown? We'll be arrested and sitting at the county jail before you can bat your eyelashes at the cops."

"Ugh!" Orrin flung himself onto the bed, then bounced back up. "We can go in through the security door on eight. They never lock it."

"Because it's on the fucking roof," I reminded him. "Orrin, please. Let's just... try and not go off half-cocked here, okay?"

He glared at me, his jaw clenching so hard I feared for his dental work. After a moment, he exhaled slowly, visibly relaxing. "You're right. Don't go off half-cocked. Maybe I...I don't know." He cast a glance about the room as if he'd find an answer hidden in the shadows. "I think I'm gonna go for a swim," he decided. "Anyone up for it?"

There was a chorus of negatives. The pool was outside and would be cold as a well-digger's ass in February right now, thanks to the overcast skies and dropping temperatures.

"Are you sure you want to go?" I asked. "Maybe we can play pool down in the game room or something?"

"I don't want to handle community balls," he announced with a hint of his old cheek. "I'm fine with cold water. I'm just going for a few laps. Then I'll be back." He rifled through his overnight bag, coming up with a clean pair of black boxer briefs and a plain t-shirt before heading into the bathroom to change. Royce, Birdie, and I all exchanged uncertain glances.

For all I know, Jim did, too, but I had no way to tell.

A few minutes later, Orrin appeared, clutching a thin hotel bath towel. "Last call?"

"I'm too tired to swim," Royce groaned. "I just want to stretch out and watch *Halloween Wars* and order a pizza."

Birdie cooed. "Extra olives, please!" he sang, throwing himself down on the bed and making it bounce under his weight.

As they fought over pizza toppings, Orrin rolled his eyes and turned to me. "Are you sure?"

"I'm sure," I promised. "Just... don't be long, okay?"

"If I'm not back in an hour," he began, then trailed off. "Well. I'll see you in a bit." Stretching up onto his toes, he pressed a quick kiss to the spot right by the corner of my mouth.

I had a weird feeling it was a goodbye.

"HE FLEW," BIRDIE ANNOUNCED about ten minutes later. "Bye bye, Ori."

"How the hell could he leave?" I demanded. "He was in his underpants and wearing flip-flops."

"The towel," Birdie said. "He wrapped his pants up in it. And he took the keys off the dresser while we were arguing about pizza toppings."

"And you waited to say something *why*?" I demanded, lurching to my feet. "Christ, how the hell—"

"I waited because Jim is with him," he replied calmly. "And Jim says it's fine. Plans change." As a heavy knock fell, he pulled out his wallet and headed for the room's door. "Besides, I'm starving and want my pizza first. He's not going to die before we have pizza." He held up a hand to silence us before answering the door and paying the delivery driver, making small talk about the weather and the restaurant.

I wanted to grab the boxes of pizza and slam the door in the driver's face, even though I knew that was my own anxious impatience talking. I glanced at Royce. "How can you be so calm?"

"I'm really not," he said quietly. "I'm waiting for an opening, and then I'm going to shake him a little."

"That's assault," Birdie singsonged, shutting the door and brandishing the boxes of pizza at us. "But I know you meant it in a metaphorical way, so I'm not gonna be upset with you." He set the boxes on the desk and popped them open. "Besides, like I said, he's not gonna die before we have dinner."

"No, but you might," Royce snarled before I could. "I'm not letting my best friend do something so phenomenally stupid—"

"Fine, fine," Birdie shouted. "We'll go!"

"He has the keys!" Royce shouted back.

"Not all of them!" Birdie pulled a single key from his hip pocket. "The rental company gave us two keys for the moving van and the SUV, just in case. Here." He tossed it at me. "You drive. You've earned it." He grabbed one of the boxes of pizza from the desk and shook it at us. "And neither of you are welcome to share my olive-pineapple goodness. Olive-pineapple goodness is for patient people."

Chapter Fourteen

ORRIN

There were several floors of labs at HEEL, most bog-standard stuff for our area of research. They were all secured, and you had to go through an entire song and dance routine to get in, but the lab on eight was different. It was the R&D lab, where all the latest and greatest tech for boosting and strengthening magical abilities was created and went through the first round of soft testing.

It was where they'd figured out how to get the nanotech to work with the magical indicators. Where they'd first created the Revive serum before I was born. The initial version had funky side effects like hair loss and severe muscle pain but, once those cleared up, left the recipient with shiny, revived magical powers.

And it was where they were working on the killswitch serum. I knew it in my bones. It was the only lab in the entire facility restricted to a specialty cohort of researchers, and it was the only lab in the entire facility under the direct and sole oversight of Calder DuMarque.

Getting into the building took over an hour. I didn't try for finesse—that wasn't in my skillset. Instead, I relied on brute force and sheer luck. The loading bay for the cafeteria, where trucks delivered crates of preprepared frozen foods for the staff to gussy up and pass off as "cooked on site" and "fresh made" had a shitty lock that broke with the application of enough force and a chunk of concrete from the parking lot.

As soon as I pushed the door open, I knew the alarms had been triggered, but I kept moving. There was no coming back from this. I thought of my dad again, my mom, the life I could have led. I thought of Sarah and Birdie and God knew how many others in the crosshairs of the lab. Of DuMarque. I felt sick, terrified. I wanted to cry. But I moved, unable to shake the feeling someone was waiting for me around every barely lit corner, following me in the shadows.

When I reached the eighth floor, I thought I heard a door open and close at the farthest end of the floor from me. My stomach cramped, and everything inside threatened to make an immediate appearance on the outside. I stood still in the thick shadows of the stairwell's recessed entrance but, after several minutes, heard nothing else. The lab doors weren't far—sliding metal doors secured with biometrics and keypads. Biometrics and keypads I could overcome with yet more brute force and a vague knowledge of wiring.

Finally making the doors give a little bit took longer than I'd hoped, but I managed to finagle them just wide enough apart to squish through. The lab itself was expansive, the overhead lights coming on as the motion detectors picked me up. Usually, people would be working, even after hours, but now it was empty and eerie, quiet save for the rasp of my breathing and the hum of machines.

A long refrigerator unit lined one of the walls, racks and racks of labeled tubes illuminated by the overheads. I padded closer. Most of the vials were common supplies used in the production of the Revive serum, but at the farthest end, behind glass doors secured with more keypads and biometrics, were rack upon rack of code-labeled tubes. Tubes I'd never seen before with pale-colored liquid inside. "Biohazard and Warning: Restricted Access" signs were taped to the doors.

The killswitch serum.

The vials sparkled dully in the orange glow from the safety lights lining the corridors. It wasn't like the movies, I thought, with blaring alarms and flashing warning lights. I knew the silent alarms had been tripped, I knew people were on the way, and I knew I wasn't going to get out in time. But the entire lab was quiet. The entire *building* was quiet.

I stood, holding my breath and straining my ears, listening for any sign of movement within the lab itself. There were so many benches and freestanding cabinets that I couldn't be sure I was truly alone. I fully expected Ivan to pop out from behind one of the shelving units or even for DuMarque to appear, rising from beneath a lab bench like the ghost of shitty choices past.

I can't just stand here. I have to move sometime.

I wished what Halloran had said was true, that my ability with foresight could work on more than matchmaking, but I had never worked to develop it, so it was weak. I wasn't about to get a sudden burst of magical steroids pumping up the ability in an instant, letting me know how this was about to turn out. Instead, I had to hope. Hope and be glad I'd left Royce and Drew back at the hotel with Birdie. Hope and be glad I took their car keys with me when I slipped out for my little swim. I would feel bad about lying to them later—if I survived this.

Taking another cautious breath, I stepped out into the open, away from the safety of the security vestibule. The automatic lights swept on, flooding the lab with LED awfulness. I flailed for a pair of the safety goggles on the rack by the door, snagging one without knocking the rest over. The anti-glare coating gave me some relief from the brightness of the overheads as I moved between the two main rows of benches. Thanks to the closure of the lab for the time being, everything was packed away. No experiments were running; no equipment hummed.

The racks upon racks of serum were safe in the wall-length refrigerator with its shatterproof glass door. I peered at them, trying to decipher the labels. They had the standard lab codes for the serum itself and the date each was created, but after that was information I couldn't parse. A code known only to the creators, or possibly not even to them. Something, I thought, DuMarque created to tell the true serum from the toxin, something he would understand and could parcel out as he saw fit.

Something my father found out. Something that killed him.

I glanced around, looking for something to get the door open for me. It was locked with a keypad and biometrics tuned to the lab techs and scientists, and I didn't have time to figure out how to bypass it without getting caught. My fingerprints were already everywhere, and those silent alarms weighed heavily on me.

"It'd be too easy for y'all to have a big plug out in the open, wouldn't it?" I muttered, checking along the bottom and sides of the unit. "Or a fire axe or something..."

Deep in the building, there was a thud.

If it had been a normal workday, the sound would have been swallowed by the typical goings-on of the day, by the buzz and hum of the lab equipment and muffling voices of people going about their lives. As it was, with the facility so quiet, I could clearly hear the heavy sound of a security door slamming shut somewhere in the distance. The noise cut through the hum of silence.

"Welp. Fuck me, then, right?" There wasn't time for finesse. I cast about for something, anything, to get the doors open so I could take a few of the vials, then run like hell, but the only things available were racks of empty test tubes, a small fire extinguisher, and a few of the small centrifuges.

Oh...oh, hey...

I grabbed the nearest centrifuge, a benchtop model weighing nothing over ten pounds, and lobbed it overhead at the unit door. The shatterproof glass held, but the hinges didn't. I hit just right to squeak the topmost hinge loose from its mooring. With a small crow of triumph, I grabbed one of the other centrifuges and gave it the ol' heave-ho at the side of the door, this time intentionally. The hinge didn't give as easily, but there was an ominous creak.

That was how the security team found me, holding a centrifuge over my head, ready to lob it for a third time at the sensitive refrigeration unit as I panted for breath. "Fuck!"

"Sir, put it down. The police have been called, and you are trespassing. And destroying expensive equipment. Step away from the refrigeration unit," the guard intoned, one hand on the gun at his hip and the other on the walkie talkie clipped to his shirt. Aside, he said into it, "It's Grimm, sir. He's in Lab 1A, trying to destroy the serum storage."

"Why am I just standing here?" I muttered, shaking my head as I realized what I was doing. Or rather not doing. With a roar, I lobbed the machine at the door again. This time, the strip of metal the hinges attached to gave way. The door hung funny, not quite falling off but giving me enough room to wiggle a hand in. Enough room to fuck up the delicately calibrated temperature within the unit.

"Sir!" The guard lunged for me, but I darted aside, scrambling up and over the nearest lab bench and aiming for the fire extinguisher. It wasn't heavy enough to damage the doors, but a blast made the guard yelp and stagger back, scrubbing at his face instead of grabbing for his gun. Making a sound I couldn't even name, I threw myself toward the unit again and grabbed for the loosened door frame. I slammed my weight back, trying to bring the door with me. But, in a moment where the gods did not so much smile upon me as laugh, the entire unit pitched forward.

The. Entire. Unit.

It was slow and fast at the same time, though that might have been the head injury talking. As it tipped toward me, it moved gradually, but still too fast for me to get out of the way. I had enough time to throw an arm in front of my face, turning away. Then I was down, pinned between the edge of the shelving and the floor with barely enough wiggle room so the metal edges didn't dig into me. I couldn't free myself easily, but I could still get enough air to breathe.

Though, I realized, I probably shouldn't try too enthusiastically. Serum bottles were shattered. Logically, I knew the method of delivery was intravenous, but the idea of breathing in any fumes, of possibly getting some in open cuts or in my mouth, terrified me.

I thought of my father in his coffin, the "funny bed," looking wrong and gone.

A sob tearing from me, I squirmed, pushing with my feet until the toes of my boots caught against something solid and I could gain purchase.

Voices shouted, and something was burning,electronics sparking and sizzling away at plastic casings. I kicked out, pushing harder, until I could get my head and one shoulder clear.

The lights were sparking, small fires scattered around the lab, and all I could think was *There's no way this was my fault.*

Suddenly, DuMarque and Ivan were in my line of vision, Ivan's eyes damn near black in the flickering light. DuMarque stretched out a hand and pushed, the unit moving off me without him even touching it.

Oh...

I didn't waste time thinking. I lurched to my feet, scrambling back and away from the pair of them. The guard was down, blood pooling by his head, and I didn't know if it was due to the unit falling or something else. I didn't have time to check.

This time, DuMarque reached for me, and I felt myself lifting off the floor. I screamed, twisting and bucking, until I hit the wall behind me. My head bounced on the cinderblock, and nausea washed through me as I slid down.

I wasn't aware of much other than movement and pain. The smell of burning and blood. Someone was shouting about the vials, about killing him, and I realized "him" was me.

"Those weren't the only ones," another voice said. DuMarque. I recognized him. He sounded far away, but I knew he was holding me up, his hand on the back of my neck.

"One thousand vials," the other voice snarled. Ivan. Ivan sounding practically feral. "Decades of research! It can't be replicated!"

"Don't be ridiculous," DuMarque chided. "Of course it can. We're scientists. We keep notes, you idiot. I regret letting you attend all those festivals as a teenager. It's made you irreparably dramatic and nonsensical."

I couldn't help it. I giggled. It was wet and tasted coppery. Something in my mouth, maybe my chest, was bleeding. The hand holding my neck squeezed and gave me a hard shake. "Sorry, but this is the most low-tier super villain shit I've ever heard, and I've seen some really shitty comic book movies in my life!"

DuMarque's blow was not unexpected, pain exploding across my face and sending me reeling back. Like I said, low-tier super villain shit.

"This is a setback, not a finality," DuMarque said softly. "Ivan, call the security company. Tell them there's been an accident, and we need an ambulance. Wait for them at the main doors. I'll be with our former employee in my private office."

I was lifted again, this time without his hands, and we were moving. Smoke filled the corridor, black and acrid. DuMarque stopped us at a smooth metal door, popping open at his touch and revealing an expansive, expensively appointed office with a disturbingly arranged hospital bed in the middle.

Seriously, the man had watched way too many shitty supervillain movies.

He dropped me into an overstuffed armchair smelling of cigar smoke and bad life choices before moving to stand behind his desk, tapping a few keys on his computer and turning a smile on me. "Don't look so worried. The bed's not for you. That's for our concierge guests seeking a bit of a top-up."

"This is legit some kind of mad scientist shit," I laughed, woozy. My head ached, and I knew I had more than a few bleeding cuts. My lungs burned. Was it from the smoke or being caught under the fallen unit? "Who started the fire?"

DuMarque rolled his eyes. "Ivan never could control his temper. He's been doing so well lately, too. We've been monitoring his dosage, but something must have pushed him over the edge." His smile wintry, he flicked a glance my direction. "Ah, here we are." The door to his office opened, and Mina, one of the data analyst techs, stepped in.

"Wait, I know you. Kind of. Drew's talked about you. I've seen you in the cafeteria..." I shook my head. "Oh, of course. Everyone here is evil, right? Everyone but me? Is this where I find out my own mother was behind my father's death?" The way DuMarque stared at me made everything in my body cold. "No...I was...no!"

"I'm sorry, you mistook my expression of sheer astonishment at your inability to shut the hell up for one of acknowledgement. No, your mother had nothing to do with his death. Mina?"

Mina shot me a look, something complicated and a little sad, before hurrying to DuMarque with a small metal case. "It's the last one from the safe."

"My own private reserve." He smiled. "Thank you, Mina. Wait around for a bit, would you? Let the team clear up in the lab before heading out. Last thing we need is for you to be seen and have more questions asked. This place is supposed to be closed at the moment, no employees on site." As he spoke, he opened the padded case and produced a half-empty serum vial and a reusable metal needle straight out of someone's medfet fantasy.

Not mine, though.

Mina hesitated, then nodded. While DuMarque prepared the injection, she took half a step toward me, only to stop when he shot her a hard glare. "Mina's feeling guilty because she can be bought. Not even for a noble reason like a sick family member or paying off the debts of a loved one. No, she's merely avaricious. Aren't you, Mina? By the way, love the new car. You don't see many Aston Martins in this end of town. Vintage?"

She nodded miserably.

"And didn't you just get a new place near Rice University? Well, I say *new*. It's quite old, isn't it?" He tipped his head in my direction, lowering his voice confidentially, "Mina does like her trappings of wealth and success. The house?" He let out a low whistle. "Six-bedroom, four bath, professional kitchen... The place was built in the early 1900s, but you'd never know from how well it's been kept up." He gave the plunger on the needle a push, squirting some of the serum out and settling the air bubble. "Old fashioned, I know, but it really is the easiest way."

Fingers knotted at her waist in an agonizing tangle, Mina looked away. "I didn't know," she mumbled. "I just thought..."

"Don't make excuses, Mina. Making excuses is a weakness. And weakness makes you undeserving. Mina is one of our stand-out subjects. Not that she'd let on." I felt the push of his power against me, holding me to the chair as he approached. "She interned here after undergrad, same as your Drew. But, unlike Drew, she was more amenable to a new paradigm in magical research."

"Murdering asshole eugenicist isn't a paradigm," I said. Hell, if I was about to die, why be quiet? Not like he'd memorialize me after, tell everyone my last words were snarky and perfect. Everyone would think I died of some hidden disease like my father had. Or maybe an aneurysm or something, I thought, watching as he pulled my arm straight and swiped an alcohol swab over the injection site. "Seriously?"

"Always stay in the habit of good hygiene," he murmured, smirking at me as he pressed the needle to my arm.

No. No one is going to think I died like my father, too young and tragically ill. No one is going to find me. Or if they do, I'll be in the news for dying while attacking DuMarque or trashing the lab.

DuMarque depressed the plunger, and I gasped, the burn of the serum making me jerk away from the needle. "It won't take long, unfortunately," DuMarque said. Mina made a choked noise behind him. "Ah, at least you have someone to cry for you here, hm? Drew will miss you, I'm sure. But he'll be so very disappointed in you. And your mother..." He clicked his tongue again. "She was always more hot-tempered than your father. I was not surprised when she left the lab. What did surprise me was how she knew what we'd done and never said a word." He pulled the needle out and gave my cheek a gentle pat. "You were right about her, you know. She understood all of the risks. She just chose to ignore them."

I refused to cry. I refused to spend my last minutes letting DuMarque know how grief—for my father, hell, for my mother, too—ripped through me. I gritted my teeth so hard my jaw ached. Her body shaking, Mina had her face turned away as DuMarque cleaned up, packing away the empty vial and needle.

I laughed quietly. "I thought you were all about the hygiene. Putting away a dirty, reusable needle? If I had more time, I'd insist on getting tested, and I'd bill you for the trouble."

DuMarque snorted. Ivan chose that moment to sail into the room, sooty and grim as he took in Mina, then smiling when his gaze landed on me. "Is it done?" he asked.

"Just about."

Ivan nodded and strode across to me, bending over me where I sat. "I want you to know I don't actually hate you. I just don't like you. You're a waste of potential, and you're a threat to what is right. I wish you had used your brain more, Orrin." He tugged on the lock of hair that had fallen over my eye. "You had such potential. Your family's legacy could have been amazing, but it's going to end here, with you."

"I honestly have no response." I stared up at him. "This is so surreal. I didn't think people actually talked like this. Did you take some sort of seminar? Or do you just watch a lot of B movies with mad scientist A-plots?"

Scowling, DuMarque opened his mouth to respond, then froze. "Mina."

She lifted her face, her expression terrified and defiant. "I'm tired," she said softly. "When I agreed to be part of your task force, I thought we were doing good. I thought... I thought we were rescuing legacies." She waved a hand at me. "But you're manipulating magic. You're stripping it away from people you think are less deserving and hoarding it for yourself!"

"You can't hoard magic," he chuckled. "I'm improving it. Perfecting it. And not everyone is worthy of perfection."

Mina shot back against the wall, her head impacting it with a sickening thud. She cried out, but he didn't release her.

"What vial was that, Mina?"

"The one from your secret stash," she grinned, blood bubbling with her breath.

My heart was pounding, but fear, not the contents of the syringe, caused it. As I looked at Mina, an entire future unfurled in front of me. I saw what was about to happen to her, for her, with her. And I knew everything, every possibility, and how it would end. She was going to die. I could see it clearly. It wasn't just assuming or fearing. The vision filled my head and became the only thing I could see. She was dead; she'd died to stop DuMarque. She'd died to save me. Even though she was still breathing, it was inevitable. Her entire body was shutting down, and I could hear her death rattle in my ears even before she drew the breath. She'd gifted me with Knowledge. She'd been unable to tell me—or anyone—everything in time, so she made sure I could see it. My head buzzed with knowledge, with...Knowing.

"What was *in* the vial?" I asked quietly.

In everything I had Seen, Mina never made it out of this room.

And she knew it.

She smiled, blood bubbling through her teeth and eyes rolling back. "It wasn't the killswitch. It was Revive."

DuMarque dropped her. She landed with a heavy thump and didn't move again. Ivan roared something incomprehensible, lunging for me even as I rolled over the arm of the chair. The Revive burned through my system, powering on links I didn't know were there, things my body had forgotten, things I thought it never had. My head ached, and I thought I might just die from this Knowing because I had no idea how to stop it, how to see what was in front of me and real in that moment and not the endless kaleidoscope of outcomes based on every tiny choice.

The tiny fraction of Knowing I'd been using for years, my little party trick, was *nothing* compared to how it felt as I looked on Ivan, on DuMarque, and saw a dozen possibilities for every choice they made as they made them.

As Ivan lunged for me, DuMarque grabbed the metal case. I saw what they would do next. DuMarque would club me with the case; Ivan would burn me. If I died then, they'd leave me in the lab to be found. If I didn't, DuMarque would give me an embolism, using the empty syringe to pop an air bubble into my neck, and I'd die in minutes.

I was not a fan of those options.

I saw Mina and...nothing. No kaleidoscope for her now. For a split second, the sheer *nothing* of looking at her was a relief, until I remembered why she had nothing left to see.

Ivan grabbed hold of my arm, and I burned, his palm like red-hot iron against my bare skin. I shouted, shrieked really, and tore away from him, pushing myself toward the door. The metal case bounced off the middle of my upper back, knocking me breathless. I staggered, almost fell, but I could see the options unfolding. Fall, and I would definitely die, and it would be messy and painful and terrifying. Make it to the door, and my chances improved. Outside the door would be more spinning visions, more possibilities, and I wouldn't know any of them unless I pushed.

The corridor was hazy as smoke poured down from the lab. Now I could hear alarms, the fire bells going off as the blazes Ivan had set caught hold of chemicals. Acrid fumes and the stench of toxic things bursting and catching made me choke. No matter which way I turned, I would choke, but running toward the lab would help. Heading for the stairs would be a trap.

I lurched on, Ivan tearing out of his father's private office behind me.

"Help," I called, but my voice was too weak to hear over the alarms and popping glass. There were no firefighters on site yet, but security was there, someone who would hear me if I got closer.

Hear me and help me, or just hear me?

The options were...not clear. And I didn't know if that was because the Revive was wearing off, or I hurt my head worse than I thought.

Or maybe, even with the magic in my blood, maybe the future couldn't always be Known.

Ivan's hands closed around my arms, and he jerked me back, sending us both tumbling to the floor. "You could have had everything," he growled. "You wasted so much. You could have ensured not only the success of the program but entire legacies, Orrin. And you chose to fuck it up." He flipped me onto my stomach and drove his knee into my spine, grabbing my hair to lift my head back, arching my neck at an angle so painful it hurt to breathe. "Drew might miss you, but he'll understand."

"Not really."

"Oh, for fuck's—"

Ivan didn't get a chance to finish. Birdie, god bless his dramatic heart, was rushing forward in a flurry of too many wallet chains, flapping canvas coat, and bright yellow hair, like some avenging canary. When his bare hands touched Ivan's face, Ivan howled. "Eat rage, fuck face," Birdie snarled. "Drew! He's here!"

"What...what," Ivan panted. "Oh my god, what's happening to me?"

Birdie squeezed his fingers until Ivan made a ridiculous pouty fishface. "Touch isn't just getting weird feelings from old shit, dumbass. Do you feel bad? I hope so..." Snarling, he shoved Ivan back down to the ground before turning to hold out a hand to me. "I promise I won't do that to you."

"What the Hell was that?"

Birdie smiled thinly. "I'll tell you when you're older. Let's get out of here before shit gets real."

"Understatement," I breathed, wincing as he looped my arm over his shoulders and led me back down the smoky hallway. As we reached the lab, I saw the security team was sitting in a row, facing out, apparently gobsmacked. "You?"

He nodded. "And Jim. I'm going to take the longest nap when we get back to the farmhouse," he groaned.

"I don't know if I want to kiss you, hit you, or both."

The sound of Drew's voice made me stumble. Warmth rushed through me, and, for the first time in hours, I felt something like peace. "If you play your cards right, I can make both happen so long as we have a safeword."

Drew closed the distance between us, taking me from Birdie's grasp and picking me up like I weighed nothing. "The safeword is *don't fucking run off and try to do something like this again, goddamnit.*"

"Too wordy. How about red for stop, green for go, yellow for I'm not sure?"

"How about let's get our asses out of here before the magic breaks, and the Keystone Cops in there decide to get up and follow?" Birdie snapped. "Jim can't keep them down long. He's not nearly strong enough. Let's move."

ROYCE WAS WAITING IN the rented moving van, parked next to Halloran's SUV. Like a nervous puppy, he tumbled out of the driver's seat as soon as he saw us emerge from the emergency exit.

"Get your ass back in there," Birdie barked. "We need to go! Hugs later, drive now!" Royce didn't even argue, which shocked me almost more than anything else.

He climbed back into the van, and Birdie followed, leaving Drew to help me into the SUV.

By the time we wound our way out of the labyrinthine parking structure, the flashing lights of the fire trucks shone in the canyon of buildings around the lab. We slipped through a narrow alley running between two of the older buildings, then out over a narrow strip of grass and curb and onto a residential road behind the complex.

"It's a solid three hours to the farmhouse," Drew murmured. "Try and get some sleep."

"I can't."

"You haven't tried."

"Drew..."

As we merged onto the feeder road, he glanced at me. We'd get on 610 and loop around to 45, then head out of town going north. It would take a while, most of the journey spent in the ubiquitous Houston traffic that seemed to grow in inverse proportion to the level of hurry we were in to get out of the city. After a long, tense moment, he nodded, and we were quiet for a long time.

Somewhere around Cut-and-Shoot (I promise you, it's a real place), we stopped for gas. It was rabbity, all four of us nervous and fast as I ran to pee, Royce darted in for drinks, and Birdie and Drew pumped gas. Then we traded places, Royce and I staying look out at the cars while Birdie and Drew took bathroom breaks.

Once we were back on the road again, Drew sighed. "My sister found out her baby's... Her baby has a positive test."

I nodded. "I figured."

"Oh?"

"Don't give me that look. I don't have some sort of sixth sense about other magicals or something. I just...figured. The way you described her made her sound hella nervous, and, frankly, the way our luck has been going lately, of course your sister would be carrying a magic baby while her fiancé is the biggest bigot on basic cable. And yeah, I did just make that about me, didn't I?" I sighed. "I only meant I'm not surprised. I think...no, I know there's way more of us than people know, and the tests HEEL was using? Those can't be trusted."

Drew drummed his fingers on the wheel. Outside, we were past the big cities and medium-sized towns, speeding along the darkened freeway with only the occasional brightly lit billboard to break up the darkness. In case you were wondering, there's a truck stop outside Huntsville very proud of having a chapel *and* an adult theater.

"Halloran said he could help her, if she wants to get away from Vick."

I stayed quiet. This didn't need my input. No matter how much I wanted to ask if he'd made sure his sister accepted.

"She's... she's afraid." He watched the taillights of the moving van in front of us. Whenever we passed under streetlights or those brightly lit billboards, I could make out the shape of Birdie's and Royce's heads as they moved and adjusted, turned to talk to one another. A blurry part of my brain thought *yes,* but I couldn't parse out why, if it was my little party trick, the remains of Revive, or merely tired thoughts.

"She's afraid," he repeated, sounding tired, "but she's going to accept."

"Yes," I hissed, giving a tiny fist pump. Drew smirked. "Sorry. I just...worry, I guess. I don't know her, really, but she's your sister. And no one should have to live afraid."

"Well, I don't know what Halloran is going to do for her, but the primary concern is making sure she has a safe place to give birth. She's due pretty much any second, and Vick's been going off the rails about that test result. He's terrified people are going to find out, and he's demanding Dee get retested. She's afraid he might do something to her or the baby."

We fell quiet again. And I did drowse a bit, but it was fitful and unpleasant. By the time I woke up, we were stopping in front of the farmhouse, and it was nearly dawn.

Chapter Fifteen

DREW

The drive to the farmhouse was angry-quiet. So was the shower when we got there. Orrin stood in the middle of the enormous bathroom, shedding his clothes with economical movements sending tiny shards of broken glass tinkling to the floor. I reached to help brush him off, but he glared until I stepped back, hands lifted to show I wouldn't reach for him again unless he asked. As he undressed, I turned the shower on and grabbed a towel from under the sink. Orrin kicked his pile of clothes toward the hamper and, smoke-smudged and bleeding from a dozen or more tiny cuts, stepped under the rain showerhead and closed his eyes.

"Well?" he asked after several long moments of standing quietly under the pouring water while the grime and blood sluiced off his chest and limbs. "Are you getting in, or are you going to wait for a formal invitation?"

I was less restrained in getting naked. It wasn't sexual—not entirely. I was just desperate to feel him against me after the past day (was it only a day? It felt terrifyingly longer) of being apart. Of not knowing what we'd find when we finally tracked him down. Still, I stood as far from him as the shower would allow. Even though it was spacious by most standards, we were still close enough for awkwardness to seep in as we stood, naked and wet and exhausted, facing one another without touching.

"Are you going to hug me or not?" His voice was so quiet, I almost lost it under the sound of the water falling. As it was, it took my brain an extra half second to parse what he'd asked, long enough for his face to crumple before I could step forward and fold him into my arms, against my chest.

His heart beat heavy against my ribs, his breath shaking with each exhale against my throat. We stood under the seemingly unending supply of warm water until a loud thump sounded from elsewhere in the house, reminding us that the others were back, too, and would also likely want to clean up. We padded out into the dimly lit hallway. The gray-yellow light of dawn peeked through the curtains, making us both look cadaverous. My stomach lurched at the thought of Orrin dead one day, like the people we found at the lab.

The number he was nearly among.

"Come on," I said, the words coming out gruff and thick. I took his hand, and he laced his fingers through mine, sending a tendril of relieved pleasure through me. He wasn't cutting himself off again. Not entirely, anyway.

I led him to our bedroom. The bed was as we'd left it just yesterday, though it felt like years—half-made and with the pillows piled up on one side and the comforter bunched awkwardly where we'd sat, talking.

Gently, Orrin shook himself free from my grasp and dropped his towel, uncaring. He padded to the chest of drawers and rummaged out a pair of his briefs and stepping into them, all without acknowledging me. Finally, after he'd rearranged the pillows and stretched out on the bed, the sheets pulled up over his chest and his body twisted into that half-pretzel shape he seemed to find most comfortable for sleep, he looked over at me blearily. "Are you coming to bed?"

"You're full of questions tonight." I tossed my own towel into the clothes basket before grabbing his off the floor to join it. I slept naked and didn't feel like changing anytime soon, sliding into the sheets beside Orrin and grabbing the comforter to keep the slight chill of the autumn morning off us.

"Only important ones," he slurred, already three-quarters of the way to sleep.

In the slowly brightening room, he slept hard against my chest, his fingers curled like a child's in rest. His entire body bore marks of what happened at HEEL, of his life falling apart and getting put back together in a strange way that would take him a while to make sense of.

I wanted to help him, be part of that with him, but I didn't know how to ask without making it seem like I was being dismissive or reductive. Snuffling, he pushed closer to me and slung his leg over my hip as he burrowed his face against my chest.

This was so close to what I'd fantasized about for weeks, months even, but at the same time a million miles away from it. I had him in my arms, and I was in his, but it wasn't the hazy-soft, idyllic world I'd imagined for us. It was terrifying around the edges, the ground in danger of shifting when we least expected it.

And I wanted us to be together when it did. I wanted to be the one to hold him up and wanted him to be the one to help me if I fell, too.

I wanted...

My brain gave a too-warm, lazy lurch.

I wanted to sleep, I decided, finally closing my eyes as someone—Royce, I think—opened the door to check on us. They stood for a minute, whoever it was, but softly closed it and let us sleep for the rest of the morning.

"GOOD MORNING!"

Birdie looked up from the bowl of...something gray that smelled like salt, a thing I was not sure was even possible before I saw how he ate and glared at Orrin. "It's one in the afternoon. And there's nothing good about it."

Orrin flashed a smile at Birdie before making a beeline for the coffeemaker. "There's plenty good about it. Caffeine, for example. And showers. And—"

"And when do you have to get your driver's license changed to show you live in the state of denial, or can you just keep your Texas one?" Birdie asked around a mouthful of his glop.

Orrin poured himself a cup of the too-strong coffee before padding to stand by my chair, leaning against me like a cat. "I woke up nauseated." When Birdie opened his mouth to give a no-doubt snarky reply, Orrin gestured for him to stay silent. "I woke up with a dozen cuts all over my body oozing blood. I woke up smelling like burning skin and chemicals, even though I showered it all off last night. I woke up angry and terrified and...and then I wanted coffee. And I wanted Drew."

"So, what? You're gonna Mary Sunshine your way through life now? Tra la tra la, my life as I knew it is ruined, but hey, I got a cuppa joe and a hot guy so it's all good!" Birdie snorted, pushing his bowl away and getting to his feet, raking his fingers back through the tangle of hot pink hair in his face. "Fuck that noise, Orrin. You don't get to live like you're ignorant of what's happening to people like us! You don't get to Mister Rogers this shit!"

"First of all." Orrin set his mug down and pushed away from me. "You take Mister Roger's name out of your mouth. Second of all, you didn't let me finish. I'm in a good mood because I have a plan. And," he added, moving closer to Birdie and lowering his voice, "it's a fucking great one."

I groaned. "Okay, no disrespect, but the last great plan you had got us fired, made us the subject of a national manhunt by a shady organization, and, oh yeah, blew up the fucking lab." Orrin turned wide eyes to me, looking both startled and a little hurt. "Sorry," I sighed. "But am I wrong?"

"No, but can you think of any other way that would have ended? Unless you'd rather us have just...pretended none of this was going on." Orrin looked back at Birdie. "Halloran said he's taking care of our stalkers, right?"

Birdie grunted. "Allegedly."

Orrin nodded. "Then all we can do right now is wait."

Expression morphing from confused to incredulous to angry, Birdie looked between Orrin and me. "Are you high, Orrin? Did you take some funny pills from the lab as a souvenir?"

Orrin shrugged. "No. I just think we need to wait."

"For *what*?" Birdie demanded. "Christ, Orrin—"

Royce slammed open the front door and called out, "Hey, guys! Guess what?"

Birdie clamped his mouth shut, and Orrin positively beamed. "Wait for Royce. Duh."

"When did he even slip out?" Birdie looked at me as if I'd have the answer.

"I have no clue. I was asleep till like half an hour ago," I reminded him. "You're the one who was up all night."

"Up all night but not staring at Royce," he muttered.

"Not the entire time anyway."

The glare Birdie shot Orrin could've flayed a man.

Royce waved a package in the air, a thick envelope wrapped in enough strapping tape to require a knife to open if I had to guess. "I found it. Just where you thought it'd be, Orrin."

"I'm so smart." Orrin moved past me to perch on the edge of the table as Birdie made a grab for Royce's...well, package.

Royce danced back out of range and headed for the desk in the den. "The place was crawling with cops and some of your brother-in-law's buddies," Royce said as he passed me. "But they didn't look twice when I flashed that card Halloran gave us and said I was from the Department of Homeland Security."

I snorted. "Remind me again why Charmers aren't considered more dangerous."

"Because they sound so damn cute." Birdie watched intently while Royce carefully cut open the package. As he peeled back the paper, an oxblood leather cover cracked with age and riddled with mildew appeared. "Oh, my God...I think I just came in my pants," Birdie gasped.

Royce made a face. "That took way less effort than I thought."

Birdie spun and faced Orrin. "How?"

Looping his arm through mine, Orrin grinned. "Something my mom said. Dad always felt like he needed to protect me with roots. She always thought it meant knowing our family history, the history of magic users and how we came to be, what happened over the centuries." He shook his head. "My dad wasn't that philosophical. But he did like a good, bad pun. Roots." He tapped the book cover. "He buried the codex under the oak tree at their old house. "

"Roots," I groaned. "Oh, my God. I wish I could have met your dad just so I could tell him that was terrible."

"Next time we hear from Jim, I'll ask him to pass it on." Birdie's expression was distracted even as he smiled.

"Jim's a medium now, on top of everything else?" I asked incredulously.

Birdie snorted. "No, but he's really into that show on The UnReality Channel with the cute medium and his butch geek boyfriend." He shrugged. "He's been dying—no pun intended—for a reason to contact the show and ask to arrange a séance." At the look on my face, he laughed, padding over to the table and peering at the thick book sitting on top of the scarred, blond wood. "This is real, though? Really real?" Birdie was so excited he was practically vibrating, his hands hovering just over the book cover. If he touched it, he'd know for sure about its veracity. It was like he couldn't allow himself to be disappointed if he was wrong, if it was nothing more than a copy Orrin's dad had found and not the real thing.

"It's really real," Orrin promised. "The Grimms have had it for decades. I don't know where it came from originally, but my father got it from his father, who got it from his mother. And now you have it."

"*We* have it," Birdie said fiercely. "We all do." He hesitated a moment more, then swooped up the book with a sharp cry, both pained and joyful. "Oh my God, all these people...it's so much..." Closing his eyes, he pressed his forehead against the mildewed cover. "I need some time. I need to shield and...oh, my god..."

Royce stared after him as he staggered to the back room where he'd set up shop. "He's so weird."

Orrin huffed a small laugh. "Come on. Let's see if there's any pizza in Halloran's deep freeze of doom."

They headed together for the garage and the freezer, leaving me in the middle of the den with the sounds of Birdie exclaiming over the codex, of Orrin and Royce rummaging for food, the crickets and the birds I could hear through the window. *We're going to be okay*, I thought, peace settling over me with a certainty I hadn't felt in years. *One way or the other, we're going to be okay.*

Epilogue

ORRIN

"Brian?"

"No."

"Bryan?"

"What? That's the same name. No."

"It's not the same! One has a *y*, one has an *i*."

Birdie lifted his head from where he'd been bent over one of the carefully preserved pages from the Star Codex. "Orrin, come get your friend. I think he's got a wire loose or something."

Royce stretched out on the purple velvet couch he'd co-opted for his own. "I'm trying to guess his name. No one calls their kid Birdie."

"I don't know, Royce. Let's ask your friend Orrin about people naming their kids weird things." Birdie made a half-assed salute in my direction. "No offense."

"None taken. It's not like Royce has room to talk. His middle name is—"

"Shut the fuck up," Royce hissed, throwing one of the small decorative pillows in my direction. "We do not speak the ancient word upon pain of most heinous death!"

Hiding a grin, Birdie ducked his face back down, pretending to study the codex as he not-too-sneakily watched Royce sprawl. Birdie would probably not admit it anytime soon, but at least some of his flirting was real when it came to Royce.

"Any progress?" I asked, nudging Royce's knees to one side so I could perch next to him. Drew would be back any moment, and I was anxious to see him again, though I tried to be cool about it.

I was failing miserably, judging by the grins both men sent my way.

With a sigh, Birdie rocked back in his chair, letting his head tip back and the bright blue (for now) hair that was usually in his face flop back. "Nothing to write home about. After 1402, the records get hella repetitive until around 1780 or so, but the science was so shitty, it's hard to parse out what was really going on from fanciful bullshit." He rocked forward, shuffled the pages gently before finding what he was looking for. "For example, 'Madame Kimborough, late of Woldsley, hath evidenced signs of the celestial affliction.'" He paused, grinning widely. "I gotta admit, I really like that phrase. I think I'm gonna start telling people I have the celestial affliction. Anyway, Madam Kimborough, according to Lord What's-His-Nuts, was purported to, and I quote, 'harshly cry out at late hours and scare the cows from milking.' Also, she apparently transformed a passable blancmange into something 'vile and crude,' but frankly, as someone who has had more than his share of blancmange, I feel like this is an oxymoron."

"It also sounds like a witch hunt," I sighed. "Was there anything else about Madame Kimborough even vaguely useful?"

"I'm sure Mister Kimborough thought so," Birdie muttered. "Ah, here's where the alleged science happens. 'Madame Kimborough comes from a magical stock. Pater was known to transform matter with barely a touch. Mater was gifted with future sight. Madame Kimbrough herself was once believed to have a touch of both abilities but, upon rigorous testing, remains as mundane as you or I.' Speak for yourself, asshat. He goes on to enumerate the rigorous tests, which include things inspired by the Inquisition. Madame Kimbrough was apparently the first of many test subjects for Lord Halsey. Who," he paused dramatically, "was not even a real lord."

"Dun dun duuuuuuuuun!" Royce cried. "So, what does this have to do with anything in the codex? I thought it was all about the history of the Star Fall and how they—er, y'all—were affected?"

"It is. There's more. Lord Halsey, or as they apparently knew him in less refined circles, Robert Richter, engaged in some rather vile practices. Like breeding humans to produce stronger magical lines."

My stomach lurched. I thought of Drew's sister and her baby—which was where Drew had gone earlier, to be with Dee at the private hospital Halloran had arranged. Birdie and Royce were both giving me similar, intense looks. "What happened to the people Richter...manipulated?"

"It wasn't all manipulation, apparently. Some of the, er, participants did so willingly, hoping to increase their family's standing in magical communities or their own status through their children. But others..." Birdie trailed off, suddenly looking uncomfortable.

"He was like me, wasn't he?" I asked quietly. "He used his abilities for...for pairing people off instead of making love matches."

"Maybe some of them did fall in love." Royce reached for my arm before letting his hand fall back to his lap, catching on fast that I didn't exactly want comforting at that moment. I was too angry, too sick about something that happened centuries ago but felt more personal than I could have ever imagined.

"I didn't think there were many like us," I finally murmured. "Madame Kimbrough's mother allegedly had foresight, right? Is that the same thing?"

"I don't know," Birdie admitted. "There was a lot of variation in the terminology until around the mid-nineteenth Century. Then there was a recodification around the end of World War One. Plus another in the early eighties when everyone wanted to push hard on the more scientific aspect of the revival projects, in the hopes people would fund them. As the lines weakened and combined, it became harder to name things." He shrugged again. "What Richter called foresight could have been sheer talent at cold reading. Or she might well have possessed some version of the ability you have. While Richter was doing his thing, abilities like yours, or things that weren't overt, were often ignored or written off as frivolous in favor of something showy, aimed at the division of classes in the case of Richter's world, or funneled into the military."

"Napoleon's mages," Royce said sagely. "Remember our eighth-grade project about how he had the mages in his troops learn from the mages in Cairo and brought more Egyptian magic to Europe?"

I snorted. "I remember you wearing the gold Pharaoh hat and doing that stupid dance to the Bangles."

"It was a *classic* song! *Walk Like an Egyptian* will always be in the top ten!" I nudged him again, aiming for his arm but hitting his ribs. We devolved into a wrestling match until Birdie cleared his throat loudly. "Sorry," I muttered. "Anyway..."

"Anyway, the codex is...a mess, basically. Ignoring the fact that it's not a true codex but a collection of bits of other codices and ephemera, it's..." He sighed. "It's a pain in the ass, is what it is, and it's been through so many hands and so many spells that my ability is barely working on it." He wiggled his fingers in a sort of morose jazz hands movement. "I feel like there should be a little blue pill for this."

The soft chime of the grandfather clock made us all jump. "Fuck," Royce sighed. "I guess I'm starting dinner."

"What? Not ordering out?" Birdie shot to his feet. "I demand proof that you can cook. I think you're a liar."

"I burned toast *one time*," Royce grouched, but didn't object as Birdie followed him into the farmhouse's old kitchen.

"HOW'S DEE?"

Drew's arrival hadn't really awakened me so much as jostled my uneasy doze. I felt heavy and sticky with the heat seeping in from around the poorly pointed windows and humidity the attic fan barely touched. But even if the temperatures had been lower, I doubted I'd have slept until Drew got back. Despite Halloran's assurances the house was safe and the precautions taken to make sure Drew wasn't followed to and from the hospital, worry gnawed at my gut until I felt him slide under the sheets and tug me against his bare chest.

"She's fine," he whispered against the side of my neck. "I have a niece. Her name is Bella Marie Hicks, and she has her mother's lungs, and, from the looks of things, she unfortunately has the Hicks nose."

"Hey." I wiggled back against him, "I like the Hicks nose! It looks good on the Hicks face. And the Hicks mouth..."

"What about the Hicks mouth?"

"I can think of a few places it'd look *real* good."

Drew chuckled against me, the burr of his stubble and huff of his breath sending delicious frissons down my back. The sensations pooled low in my belly before slipping downward in a warm rush. I arched my hips back, feeling Drew's half-hard cock slip against the curve of my ass before we managed to slot together more comfortably. Bringing him to full mast didn't take much, the broad head of his cock nudging the back of my balls. "If you slept naked like I do," Drew murmured, "I wouldn't have to stop what we're doing for you to take off your underwear."

"If I slept naked like you do, I'd startle the hell out of Royce whenever I got up to pee in the middle of the night. Between his insomnia and how the toilet shrieks like a banshee when you flush, he'd definitely get an eyeful of your favorite bits."

"It's a trade I'm willing to make," he said gravely, covering my mouth with his.

I burst into laughter, swallowing the sound as it turned into a groan when his hand slipped beneath the waistband of my briefs and traced soft lines up and down my cock. "Halloran's not back till Tuesday, Royce is in his room on the other side of the house, and Birdie's light was out, so he's either asleep or whatever it is he does when he sits in the dark and stares at things."

"Mr. Hicks," I demanded quietly, "are you trying to seduce me?"

He squeezed me gently. I gasped as he swiped his thumb through the bead of precum pearling on the head of my cock and used it to slick a path along the vein running along the underside of my length. "I think I'm succeeding."

My underpants didn't take long at all to go sailing across the room, landing God only knew where with a soft thump. (I sincerely hoped it wasn't on that picture of Halloran's grandmother Drew had turned to face the wall our first night in the house.) Drew's mouth worked magic on mine, leaving me gasping as he rummaged in the nightstand drawer for the almost-empty bottle of lube I'd tossed in there about a week before.

In all fairness, it was travel-sized, so it wasn't like we'd been having a ton of penetrative sex.

Blowjobs, though...

Drew's fingers slipped between my cheeks, pressing lightly over the tight furl of my hole while he ducked his head down to my chest. The first pinch of his teeth against the hard bud of my nipple made me gasp in an embarrassingly loud, high-pitched fashion. That seemed to trigger him to go all out, skipping the gentle assault he'd been heading toward. Before long, my legs were over his shoulders, and three of his long, talented fingers were buried to the hilt in my ass.

I never knew my ankles were an erogenous zone until he mouthed them each in turn while he fingered me open. "Fuck, Drew!"

"That is sincerely what I'm hoping," he murmured on a chuckle. "Look how needy you are for me, Orrin..." He punctuated his words with a curve of his fingers, brushing against my prostate and making me arch my hips, seeking more of him even as he pulled away. He didn't leave me wanting long, though. Pushing my legs back and wide, he pressed the mushroom head of his cock against my hole and slid in, slowly and inexorably.

Somewhere in the farmhouse, Royce made a vaguely disgusted noise at something or someone else. For a moment, Drew and I froze, but the giggles were unstoppable. With him fully seated inside me, I burst into a fit of laughter, at once strange and wonderful, from top to bottom (literally). Drew grabbed my legs tighter and bent to press a kiss to my calf, his own soft laughter tickling my skin. I didn't have time to linger on the pleasant, soft sensation, though.

He pulled my legs together and fucked in earnest. The combination of the shift in position and the way everything felt tighter, harder, *more* pushed me closer to the edge than I wanted at first. But seeing Drew's head thrown back as he panted my name, the corded muscles in his neck as he tried to keep quiet while his body shook with pleasure and need... I closed my eyes and let go.

My release pulsed out of me, splattering my stomach, my chest, my throat. With the physical came the magical. A pulse of magic stirred through my body, a cool wave of understanding deeper than simply knowing. That funny watermelon taste danced on the back of my tongue as magic sparked along every nerve ending in my body. Drew's shuddering climax lit that cool wave on fire as his energy washed over mine and, for a moment, tangled together with it.

Gently, he pulled free of me, and the warm rush of his spunk dribbling from my body made me shudder. He murmured something unintelligible, flailed at the nightstand for a moment, and returned with a handful of tissues to aid in cleanup. "I'm going to be covered in papery bits," I said quietly. "I'll look like a half-plucked chicken."

"My half-plucked chicken," he muttered, already drowsy. He pulled me against his chest, back in the position that started it all, and was soon snoring against the back of my neck.

I must be in love when even his snores make me happy.

THE NEXT FEW DAYS PASSED in fits and starts. Long periods of dull nothingness while Birdie ensconced himself in his room to go over documents when Halloran was gone and Drew went off to sit with Dee and Bella. Then sudden bursts of activity after Birdie would find something potentially helpful about this subtle ability or that one and race off to contact Halloran about another lead to follow, another line to trace.

A few times, I reached for my phone, thinking to call Mom and let her know I was alive, that I was okay, but then I'd remember what almost happened to me—to *us*— and I'd sink back into the sofa, or the bed, or, in one case, the patch of carpet by the TV stand and mope.

Before I leave here, I'll ask Halloran to contact her. I wondered who he'd use this time, if he had any Vessels still out there willing to help him since the fight at HEEL.

"Did you know," Royce said on Tuesday morning while we all pretended not to be waiting for Halloran to return, "apparently you were fired due to your part in an industrial espionage campaign?" He glanced up from the tablet he'd borrowed from Birdie. "Very affecting piece in the *Herald* about how you had such promise and how your parents were once the apple-cheeked darlings of the lab, but you were a viper taken into their bosom and—"

"It does not say that!" I grabbed the tablet from Royce and scanned the article. "Oh my God...they *paid* someone to write this? This person went to school for journalism and everything?"

"More likely HEEL paid someone to write it," Birdie pointed out. He'd emerged from his hideaway, now sporting a shock of acid-green hair, and was perched on one of the kitchen stools, eating a bowl of grits with either too much or the perfect amount of gravy, depending on your point of view. "There's no such thing as fair and balanced reporting. At least not in the big media companies. You want to know the truth, look to the indie folks, the guerilla journalists."

"Cynical," Royce chided. Birdie raised a brow. "You're not wrong, but you're still cynical."

"How can I be cynical if I'm right?" Birdie demanded, and they were off on another pick-pick-pick argument.

They were still at it an hour later when Halloran came back, followed in the door by Drew. "Children," Halloran chided. "Behave or you don't get your prezzies."

"Please never say prezzies again," Birdie demanded, switching his attention from Royce to Halloran in a neat pivot. "And look what you dragged in. Drew, I thought you were helping Dee get settled today."

"Taken care of." Drew darted a glance my way. "That's kind of something we need to talk about, actually."

Halloran held up a hand, quieting us all. "First, lunch. I'm tired of hockey puck drive-through burgers." He pushed past Royce and Birdie, shot me a quick smile, and headed for the kitchen. He refused to talk about his trip until he'd put one of the frozen lasagnas from the deep freeze in the oven and directed Drew to make a pitcher of sweet tea. "With actual sugar, for god's sake, none of that monk fruit shit I know Birdie's been sneaking in on me."

"Now," he sighed once the food was underway and the tea was steeping, "we talk. Drew, would you like to go first?"

We all knew that was not so much a question as a direction. Drew nodded. "Dee's going to be living in a safe house. Bella's test was a very strong positive..." Drew looked shaken, angry. For a moment, I felt a flare of uncertainty, burning hot despite the fact I *knew—Knew—*we were meant to be. Something showed in my expression because Drew closed the distance between us and pulled me into an embrace. "It's not because of that," he murmured. "It's Vick."

Halloran had pity on him and took over. "The hospital Dee was at is friendly to our particular cause. They use testing protocols developed by me and Reynard, which have a much higher degree of accuracy than the standard tests, and the staff is largely empathic. In the magical sense," he added unnecessarily. "Not the witchy woo-woo sense."

Royce rolled his eyes. "Splitting hairs there," he muttered under his breath, only to get elbowed by Birdie and me at the same time.

"The staff confirmed what the test showed. Bella is quite strongly magical. And, as Dee feared, Vick was attempting to get to her and his daughter overnight. The security procedures in place thankfully prevented him, as did Dee's restraining order, but we," he nodded at Drew, "felt it was time to get Dee and Bella somewhere safer."

"She's, um...she's going to be staying with someone who has a lot of experience keeping magical kids safe. Well, at least one magical kid," Drew said sheepishly.

And I knew. I *knew* without magic. "My *mother*?"

Halloran smiled brightly. "Eloise is the perfect choice. Not only does she have a wealth of experience living hidden in plain sight, she loves kids and," he added with a pointed look in my direction, "she wanted to remind you she kept your scrawny ass alive even through your parkour phase, so a baby should be no problem."

"My mother is one of the first places they'll look," I snapped. "Christ—"

"No, she isn't." Royce spoke this time, an amused expression dancing over his features. "As far as everyone knows, y'all had a falling out. A huge one. Like Olympic-sized. You destroyed an entire lab out of anger over her choices regarding how you were raised."

Nodding, Halloran brandished oven mitts at Royce. "Bingo. And as a reward, you get to take the food out and start dishing it up. Now." He turned to me with a clap of his hands. "Your mother loves you. And she knows you're hurt and angry and a thousand other things. And trust me, I do, too. But we—and I hope you—also know your father's wishes for you to embrace who you are, his attempt to keep you safe... It was not a choice he made lightly. He knew what might happen, but he wasn't easy with the decision, Orrin. Your mother is doing this for him as much as she is for you and Drew."

"What...what do you mean?" I shook my head. "How is this for my father?"

"He wanted future generations to be safe, Orrin. He wanted kids like you to grow up owning their magic, to be just as valued as those with stronger powers, more socially impressive abilities. Protecting Bella from Hayden and his collection of asshats is one thing your mother can do to honor that. She and Dee are setting up house right now, in one of the lab's safehouses. They have a Changeling with them, strong enough to hide them when they go out."

A Changeling? That drew me up short. They were rarer than someone like me, if I remembered Birdie's little flowchart correctly. He'd proudly showed it to us a few nights previously, "What's that?"

"The original appearance of magic in the world," he said, tapping the X with his finger. "We don't know for sure who the first person or people were to manifest openly, or what those powers were. But we do know that here," he indicated the first row beneath the X, "we have people demonstrating the Big Two, telekinesis and telepathy, in the mid-1400s. And here," he tapped the next line, "less than a hundred years later, they were already differentiating between subtypes. Touch, Sight, Knowing, and so on."

The chart was remarkably detailed, even listing one-offs and combination abilities. Changelings had been starred, along with Ghosts, or people like Jim who had somehow managed to attain invisibility. Those were more rare than Changelings and had not been noted in about two centuries, save for Jim, who was the only one who'd never managed to undo the invisibility and the only one who'd gained the ability due to inorganic means. But Changelings... They'd been rare as hen's teeth well into the modern times and often feared due to the nature and strength of their powers. And now one was with my mom and Drew's sister and niece.

"I want to see my mom." I was surprised to hear the words coming out. "I need to..."

Halloran laid a heavy hand on my shoulder. "We'll figure out a way soon, son...er, Orrin. We'll figure it out. Now. Food. And then, some news."

"More?" I groaned, letting Drew lead me to the table where Birdie had set out plates and Royce was dishing out slabs of pasta and veggies.

"Mmm. I think you might like this. I know you've been bored lately; I didn't have to be here to know you'd be climbing the walls." Halloran paused to take a bite of his food, then wash it down with a sip of tea in what I'm sure was a little push of control to remind us who was in charge.

Technically.

"I have a job for you and Drew." He smiled at us across the table like some demented patron saint of mad scientists. "It seems our recent activities have stirred up quite a hornet's nest. The lab has been contacted several times over the past few days by magicals seeking help."

Staring at Halloran, Drew was decimating his lasagna with the tines of his fork but not eating a single bite. "What does that have to do with us?"

"Well, I hired you after HEEL fired you, didn't I? I want you to do your jobs. Go out and find these people. Bring them to me." He grinned again. "No rush, though. You can start after lunch."

Royce choked on a disbelieving laugh. Birdie nodded, though I'm not sure if he was agreeing with Halloran, Royce, or both. I looked at Drew, and he shrugged.

"Well," he said, finally digging into his food, "time's wasting."

Where am I...

The best place to find links to my books, updates, teasers, newsletters, and new release info is via my website:

www.booksbymeredith.com

You can also find me on social media at:

www.facebook.com/groups/meredithsreadingranch

www.twitter.com/meredithspies

www.facebook.com/meredithspiesauthor

www.instagram.com/meredithspies

Coming Soon...

BUMP IN THE NIGHT (Medium at Large Book One) *MM Paranormal Romance, February 2020*

Science of Magic Book 2 *March 2020*

About the Author

MEREDITH LIKES TO WRITE about sexy stuff, weird stuff, and sometimes weird stuff doing sexy stuff. Originally from Texas, they live elsewhere now with their family and two cats who think they are gods (in fact, they're pretty sure of it). Meredith writes queer-centered romances in various subgenres including paranormal, speculative fiction/alternate universe, contemporary, and historical.They firmly believe in happily ever afters and that there is no reason anyone should wear socks with open toe shoes.

For sneak peeks at upcoming works and other goodies, check out Meredith's Reading Ranch (the reader group,) website, or other social media.

CPSIA information can be obtained
at www.ICGtesting.com
Printed in the USA
LVHW040130090121
676048LV00005B/196

9 780578 830322